SILVER FOX'S TWIN SURPRISE

LYDIA HALL

ALSO BY LYDIA HALL

Series: Holiday Hearts

Merry Mix-Up || Christmas in His Arms || Single Dad's Christmas
Cookie

Series: Off Limits Doctors

Silver Fox's Secret Baby || Silver Fox's Intern Dilemma || Silver Fox's
Twin Surprise

Series: Spicy Office Secrets

New Beginnings || Corporate Connection || Caught in the Middle ||
Faking It For The Boss || Baby Makes Three || The Boss's Secret || My
Best Friend's Dad || Corporate Heat

Series: The Wounded Hearts

Ruthless Beast || Merciless Monster || Devilish Prince || Relentless

Refuge || Vicious Vows || Lethal Lover || Sinister Savior || Wicked Union

Series: The SEAL's Protection

Guarded by the SEAL || Protected by the SEAL || Saved by the SEAL || Rescued by the SEAL

Series: The Big Bad Braddock Brothers

Burning Love || Tell Me You Love Me || Second Chance at Love || Pregnant: Who is the Father? || Pregnant with the Bad Boy

Series: The Forbidden Attraction

My Mommy's Boyfriend || Daddy's Best Friend || Daddy Undercover || The Doctor's Twins || She's Mine || Tangled Trust || Passion || Got to be You

Series: Corrupt Bloodlines

Dangerous Games || Dangerous Refuge || Dangerous Obsession || Dangerous Vengeance || Dangerous Secrets

BLURB

I never meant to fall for the brooding surgeon with storm-gray eyes.

They warned me about the Silver Fox—damaged, distant, dangerous to love.

Our hidden moments became my addiction, *until the test showed positive.*

Not one heartbeat, but two—twins growing beneath my heart.

He's fighting demons he won't share, pulling away when I need him most.

My body is betraying me, my secret becoming harder to hide.

They say he almost killed a senator in surgery.

I'm carrying his babies, but he might lose everything before he knows.

How long can I protect him from a truth that's growing inside me?

Author's Note: *Brace yourself for this steamy age-gap medical romance featuring secret pregnancy, forbidden office romance, and silver fox drama that'll make your heart monitor beep!*

COLE

"Suction..." I reached out my hand to take the hemovac to suction out the remaining blood and body fluids that lingered after surgery. The patient had done well for the most part, but I was watching his vitals closely. Even during routine procedures like this hernia repair, things could go wrong.

The nurse placed the suction tube onto my palm and I clasped it, then maneuvered it to begin cleaning up the man's abdominal cavity. As I did, my hand shuddered a little, almost imperceptibly, but it was there. I noticed it. It made me wince, but I kept my head down and continued working, praying no one else saw it.

The tremors had started three months ago, only when I was very stressed or overly tired, but they were noticeable enough that I should have reported them. I kept hoping they'd go away, that it was a result of fatigue or tension, but today I wasn't feeling tired or stressed at all. In fact, I had a good weekend planned, one I was looking forward to. So the slight shiver of my hand frustrated me.

"There we go," I said, handing the hemovac back to the nurse. She took it from me and turned to replace it to its spot, then returned with my needle to suture the patient.

"Have any plans this weekend?" she asked, making conversation as was normal during any surgery. It wasn't uncommon to carry on complete conversations with nursing staff while operating. We were a great team, and we'd worked well together for several years now.

"Actually, yes," I told her. "I'm going to see the Broncos' quarterback play in the pro-bowl." I grinned beneath my PPE mask and thought of how I'd scored the tickets to the game by helping a buddy of mine with his board exams. His father had season tickets and as his former mentor, he'd asked me to help him study in exchange for the tickets. I was thrilled, but of course, I'd have helped him anyway.

"Oh, that's great. I heard the weather is supposed to be gorgeous Sunday." I could see the sparkle in her eye as I looked up at her and knew she was smiling too. But when my hand tremored again, I wasn't smiling.

I was, however, thankful she was looking up at me and not at my fingers which were tying off the first suture. The last thing I needed was one of the nurses stepping in to report me for this. It wasn't something I could hide, though it wasn't anything career ending, or at least I didn't think so. Still, if anyone doubted my ability to perform, for the safety of my patients, they had to report it.

"Yeah, I'm looking forward to it," I told her, but the conversation dropped there. I had to focus on what I was doing so I didn't make a mistake, especially with the heat already hanging over my head from that previous surgery. It wasn't a tremor that caused the mistake, but I'd never convince anyone of that. Not if they saw my hand shake the way I had.

When I finished the last suture, I sucked in a deep, cleansing breath and handed the nurse the needle. "Wrap it up and get him back to his room now. I'm going home," I told her with a tight smile. My part of this operation was done, and the patient could move to recovery, and I was ready to call it a day.

"No problem, Dr. Hastings," she said, and I backed away to let the rest of the team work.

As I walked toward the scrub room, I gripped my right hand and massaged gently. The fact that my stretches and exercises weren't working to improve what was going on was concerning. I wasn't an orthopedic doctor—I was a surgeon who specialized in trauma situations—but I knew enough to know hand tremors like this weren't good. I wasn't going to rule out something severe, but I wanted to focus on the obvious stuff that was explainable and treatable.

I scrubbed out and took off my scrub cap, tossed my surgical gown in the garbage, and headed right to my office. A few of the guys threw some jibes at me and I laughed them off, and with the on-call doctor prepped to keep tabs on my patient, I made my way to the parking garage. I needed this weekend to de-stress and relax.

For the past few weeks, the board had been investigating what happened during the surgery that almost cost the patient his life. I believed it was a clerical error, someone not informing me of the patient's routine medicines before I gave orders for other medications that posed a significant risk—which was inevitably realized on my surgical table. But without proof that someone else had made the mistake, the onus was on me to explain why he almost bled out.

I ran a hand through my hair and let the chill of the early March breeze kiss my skin as I stepped through the door into the parking garage. I'd spent too much time agonizing over what happened and how, and this weekend was all about helping me forget that and just try to relax. I took two days off and intended to spend both days detoxing from work stress and releasing tension.

My footsteps echoed across the walls of the parking garage. In the distance I heard a car moving, tires squealing quietly as it rounded the corner to rise or descend on the garage's ramps, and the stench of exhaust and oily fast food hit my nose. The scents of Denver had never changed. The bowl shape tucked into the mountains just east of the Twin Peaks the hospital gained its name from made more of a smog trap than I was sure the founders intended. Today was no different.

I walked up the ramp toward my black SUV and noticed a woman standing behind her car with her phone to her ear looking frustrated. She leaned against the car with her arms crossed over her chest and glared at the phone before grunting and shoving it in her pocket.

Her dark, wavy hair hung around her shoulders, but it had kinks in it as if it'd been tied up in a bun or pony tail for the day and had only just been let down. She wore light blue scrubs and a nametag with the hospital logo on it.

"Hi, uh..." I leaned closer and read her name aloud. "Rose..." My soft smile did nothing to lighten the scowl on her face. "Is everything okay?" Lots of people who worked here wore scrubs, but not all of them had badges like this. She was a registered nurse, and a frustrated one, by the looks of it.

"Well, I have a dead battery. I tried to call a tow truck, but they said it would be three hours. So, yeah... If you have jumper cables, I could use some help." Her soprano tone was pleasant, not grating or nasally at all. I watched her eyes flick toward her open hood and back to my face, and I grinned at her.

"You're in luck, Rose. I have a set of jumper cables, and I'm parked right over here. And all it will cost you is one smile." Her face lit up and a genuine warmth flushed her cheeks as she returned my smile with one of her own. She was radiant, glowing with gratitude as she nodded.

"Thank you," she said shyly as I turned to get my car.

I was struck by how pretty she was right away. It wasn't something I usually noticed, not after Kate died. I never looked at another woman like I did Kate. She was my one and only, and any time I even thought of moving on, I felt guilty. But I had to admit even my better judgment was tested with Rose.

I pulled my SUV up and parked next to her, then I popped the hood but left the engine running and walked to the back. She met me there as I lifted the tailgate and sorted through the odds and ends in my cargo area for the jumper cables, which I found buried in the side pocket with the jack.

"Got 'em," I mumbled, and I turned to see her still smiling.

"My gosh, you're a lifesaver. I would've been standing here forever. I'm so hungry too. I haven't eaten yet today." She followed me around the front of her car where I clamped each alligator clamp to the appropriate battery terminal on her car and the positive to mine. Then I clamped the negative to an engine mount and told her to fire it up.

Rose climbed into her car and turned the key and it fired on the first try, but in the interest of her getting home safe with headlights and her radio working, I left the cables attached for a few more seconds.

When she climbed out of her car and joined me, she was shivering. Night was taking hold and the breeze had picked up. She hugged her arms over her body, pushing her tits up in front. I noticed the curve of them and the hardness of her nipples under the layers of fabric, which wasn't something she could hide. I pried my eyes away, but not before I got a little turned on. This work stress had me off my game.

"Thank you, Doctor..." She leaned in as if trying to read my name badge, but it was clipped under my lab coat on my scrubs pocket, hidden away.

I pulled my lab coat back so she could see and said, "Dr. Cole Hastings at your service."

She chuckled, and I joined her. The tinkling of her laughter was as pleasant as the tone of her voice, and the smile on her face. If I didn't know better, I'd have said Rose was an angel sent right when I needed some sort of pick me up. It put me at ease in a way I hadn't felt in years.

"Well, Dr. Cole Hastings, I owe you big time. Maybe a coffee or something." Rose thrust out her hand and leaned on the side of her car next to the jumper cables that dangled out of her engine bay.

I shook her hand and nodded. "I like it black, and I work first shift, but I'm off for a few days." I narrowed my eyes at her and tried to place this face, but I couldn't. I knew all the nurses from surgical, but there were plenty of other departments. Still, I'd never seen her around. "Are you new around here?" I asked, and she nodded.

"Yes, actually." She pulled her hand back after I let go and tucked it around her body again in an attempt to keep herself warm. "I just got an apartment here in the city. I started at Twin Peaks two weeks ago, so I'm sort of brand-new to the city and the hospital." She nodded as she spoke, and her hair swayed. I was mesmerized by it. Like ripples of water across a pond, it drew my attention downward toward her chest again, and I internally scolded myself for checking her out.

"Well, welcome to both. It's great to have you..." I felt a little awkward. If I were in the market to meet or date a woman, now would have been the perfect chance to see if this one in particular would go to dinner. But Kate was my one and only—high school sweetheart—and when she died in that accident, I told myself I'd never move on. Maybe I'd change my mind at some point, but in the middle of a brewing scandal with a potential malpractice suit looming, it wasn't the right time.

Rose sighed happily and looked down at the engine. "Is it okay to unplug it?" she asked naively, and I chortled.

"Sure, we can remove the clamps now."

I reached for the ones on her car at the same time she did, and we both leaned in without paying attention to the other. Our heads smacked, and we both jolted back in pain, holding our heads.

6

"Oh, my God, I'm so sorry." Her face was screwed up into a wince, but all I could do was linger close to her for a second and admire how perfect her complexion was. She wore no makeup and had no jewelry, just a pure skin tone and warm brown eyes.

"I, uh... It's okay." I mumbled around for a second trying to think of words, which had somehow been knocked right out of my head by that blow, and then I nodded at her. "I can finish up..."

Rose retreated in obvious embarrassment to her car, and I thought of how strongly my body felt attracted to her. The pull of chemistry had me forgetting about Kate or the disciplinary board or even the football game. I unhooked the cables and put her hood down, then mine, and when I stopped by her open window, she winced again.

"I'm really sorry. Thank you so much for helping me. I appreciate that so much." Rose was apologetic and positively irresistible.

"It's okay," I told her. "Maybe we'll bump into each other again soon." I winked at her and she blushed, and as I strolled to the back of my SUV to put the cables away, she backed out and drove off.

I wasn't sure what just happened between us except that Rose had made me feel things no woman since Kate had. I sort of liked it. I sort of really did hope we'd bump into each other again. It was a nice feeling.

2

ROSE

I babied my little Toyota Corolla the whole way home thinking I might have problems with it again, but it really was just a dumb mistake. I'd left my charging wire plugged into the port after having given my cell a boost on the drive across town to work. I forgot to plug it in last night, so the fifteen-minute drive was all the charge I had and my forgetfulness cost me in the form of a dead battery.

Thankfully, Dr. Cole Hastings was there to save the day. And make me blush. I felt a little giddy for a few seconds after we bumped heads and he looked into my eyes like that. But it faded a little as I drove home and thought about how unlikely it was that he'd even take an interest in me. Smacking heads in a parking garage over a dead battery wasn't exactly a recipe for love at first sight.

I stopped by the market on my way home and got a few snacks knowing Alana would appreciate them. When I first moved into the city to accept the job at Twin Peaks Memorial, I didn't know where I'd live. But I met Alana on my first day after overhearing how her roommate skipped town and left her with the rent. She was a pharmaceutical rep, and since I was a nurse, we happened to be in the right place at the right time—the administrative offices of the hospital.

Now we were practically like sisters. It'd only been two weeks, but I felt like we knew each other our whole lives. We shared the car and all our living expenses, and it made accepting this job that much easier.

"I'm home," I called as I struggled through the door with the bags of groceries. I made sure to double-check that my charging wire in the car wasn't plugged in this time so I didn't head out tomorrow expecting to go to work and have a dead battery again.

"Oh, good! I'm so snacky... Did you get pretzels?" Alana bounced toward me with a grin on her face and took a few bags from my hands as I used my foot to kick the door shut. She was about as eager to eat as I was to tell her about my day. Nothing even remotely interesting had happened to me since I met her besides being vomited or peed on, and she wasn't interested in hearing those things.

"Yes, well, they came at a price." I chuckled, and she eyed me as she set the plastic sacks on the countertop. I kicked off my shoes and joined her at the kitchen counter. The simple open floorplan felt too hollow and empty at first, but I'd grown used to being able to see the living room, dining room, and kitchen the instant I walked through the front door.

"What do you mean?" Alana found the bag of pretzels and the package of peanut M&M's and claimed them as she leaned back on the counter and watched me set the other bags down.

"Oh, nothing... Just an interesting afternoon. That's all." I breathed in the scents of lilac and lavender and glanced at the candle she had burning on the peninsula that separated the counter from the dining table. It smelled good. this place always smelled good. It was either her perfume or a scented candle.

"Dish," she said, tearing open the pretzels, and I grabbed the container of Rocky Road and a spoon and turned to face her expectant expression. Her eyebrows were so high she looked like a cartoon character.

I chuckled. "Well, so after work, I went to my car to leave like normal, and when I got in the car, the battery was so dead it wouldn't even power the radio."

She deadpanned and lifted an eyebrow at me. "You got me all excited about a dead battery? Man, life in a small town must've sucked."

I laughed and snorted and shook my head as I tried to swallow the large spoonful of ice cream I'd just shoved into my mouth.

"No," I said, gasping and choking on the bite. I managed to swallow my food and wipe my mouth before continuing. "Okay, so I was sitting there with my hood up, and a hot doctor came out and helped jumpstart my car, and I definitely think he was checking me out."

She snickered and smirked, then said, "Jump your car or jump your bones?"

I rolled my eyes at her as I continued my story. "Seriously, though, he was so frickin' hot. I mean, silver fox hot. He had these blue eyes that—"

"Okay, hold on." Alana pushed off from the counter and walked over to a bar stool and sat down on the far side of the peninsula. I took a bite of ice cream and put the rest of the snacks away listening to her try to be all wise and everything. "Don't get me wrong. I totally want you to meet a super hot guy and get laid and all, but a doctor? Isn't there some sort of policy against dating coworkers? And what if he's married?"

I slid the box of granola bars onto the shelf in the cupboard next to the cereal and sighed. I hadn't even looked at his wedding ring finger, but the way he looked at me didn't say "Married—hands off." It said, "I'm prowling."

"Okay, so a girl can fantasize, right?" I tried to chuckle it off, but she made another good point.

"And besides, do you really think a silver fox wants something serious from a twenty-something? Men who rob the cradle only want sex. You shouldn't get all dreamy eyed about Dr. Hot Pants unless you know his intentions. He could've been checking you out for sex and nothing more. I'd hate to see you get hurt."

I heard the crunch of her chewing before I turned back around to steal another bite of my ice cream. Hearing those words took the wind right out of my sails. It was just crushing. I knew that, but her wisdom brought me down to Earth where my head belonged, not in the clouds.

"Okay, okay... but he was still super hot." I grinned at her and shoveled more icy confection into my mouth, and she rolled her eyes as she popped a handful of M&M's into hers.

We watched a movie and ate our snacks, and later when I finally crawled into bed, all I could think about was my single mother and how much we struggled financially when I was growing up. Dad had really hurt her, and all she wanted for me was a successful life where I wasn't dependent on any man. It was why she forced me to go to college, why she pushed me toward nursing. It paid well.

If I got roped into some fling with a silver fox who only wanted sex, I was risking my heart and potentially ending up a single mom like her. It wasn't what I wanted. I decided right then and there to at least try to stay on the straight and narrow the way Mom would expect. But if that hot doctor flirted with me, I wasn't responsible for my reaction. His grin detonated a bomb inside my body when he flashed it at me. I didn't think outright flirting would be something I could walk away from.

11

3

COLE

I walked out of my last patient's room with a bit more weight on my shoulders than I'd have liked there to be. My tablet was tucked under my arm and my stomach was growling, but the only thing on my mind was the meeting I was supposed to have with the board later today to discuss the patient who was seeking some sort of compensation for my mistake. I had no way of knowing what they'd say, which put me on edge.

After dropping my tablet in my office, I headed down toward the cafeteria for some lunch. At least that much would distract me and help me keep my mind off whatever might happen. Not knowing the future was normally never a problem because I liked to live in the moment. But this time, fear of the unknown was goading me like an invisible monster under my bed.

The cafeteria was busy, so many familiar faces. I smiled and waved as I walked past a table where a few other doctors I knew were seated. Just a glance at their lunch plates made my stomach rumble again. The smell wasn't as appetizing as the looks, but I knew the minute I bit into that pot roast, I'd be in heaven. My mouth was already watering.

The line wasn't too long, and I found myself standing there behind my friend Juan—also a surgeon here at Twin Peaks. He turned to smack my hand and bump my fist before giving me a shake. His unique handshake style always made me chuckle. It was like being friends with a teenager at times.

"Yo, man, how's it going?" Juan flashed me an award-winning smile, and I shrugged a shoulder as my eyes swept up to the menu board. Today's special was pot roast, carrots, and mashed potatoes with a roll and Jell-O for dessert. Yes, my mouth was watering.

"You know... I'm still alive, so that's something to be thankful for." The greeting was my familiar go-to phrase, and I typically meant it in a very positive way. Being thankful for things helped keep me grounded and looking at the positive. But today, it was heavy. If I really had caused that man's death, I didn't think I'd feel quite the same way.

"Hey, yeah... Breath in the lungs, blood in the veins... You got a lot to be thankful for." He winked at me and gripped my shoulder and squeezed it, then turned back to the counter and took a step forward.

"What'll it be, honey?" Marge, the cafeteria lady, with her hair net and white uniform, had thick, dark eyebrows that looked more like cater-pillars, and I thought how ironic it was that they didn't have hairnets over them too.

"Oh, Miss Marjorie, I'll have the special, please. And can I get a black coffee for that too?" He wagged his eyebrows and smiled. Juan was on his best behavior with the lunch lady, just as if we were in high school again and she had the authority to take us by the ear and drag us to the principal. Even his manner of speaking changed when he spoke to her, or maybe he only used his laid-back jargon with me because we played basketball and golf on the weekends and I beat him at every-thing and trash talked the whole time.

"Keep your butter to yourself," she said, playfully scowling. She turned to walk away and put his order in, and Juan picked up a tray and set it on the line and moved forward to wait for his food, and I stepped up to the counter and turned to him.

"Butter to yourself?" I asked, and he snickered.

"I like to butter the ladies up so I can keep them smiling... You know, it keeps everyone in a better mood, and if I can make her mood better now, then when she gets to an old curmudgeon like you, maybe my happiness will rub off onto you." His added wink—a signature Juan move—had me rolling my eyes.

"You have no idea..." I sucked in a breath to fill my lungs, hoping to release some of the tension in my chest, and Marge returned with his plate of food. Juan loaded his goodies onto his tray and Marge turned to me, but before she could ask, I said, "I'll have what he's having, but hold the coffee. Thanks."

Five minutes later, we were meandering around the cafeteria looking for a few empty chairs. We lucked out and found a full empty table all the way at the back of the room closest to the vending machines. I was glad we wouldn't have to immediately share a space with anyone else. I was too stressed out to sit around and small talk with coworkers, and Juan knew enough to leave me alone if I was grumpy.

I sat down and opened my cutlery pack, taking the salt and pepper and sprinkling them over the food. My first bite was so good I groaned in pleasure, more so because I knew this food was going to take away the gnawing ache in the pit of my stomach. Hospital food was rarely any good, but however they made this, it was at least palatable.

"So, what gives? Usually, you're pretty upbeat. Somethin' botherin' you today?" Juan shoved a huge bite of food into his mouth and chewed, and I sighed and again lifted one shoulder in a shrug.

"I don't know." I sighed and glanced around. No one was close enough to hear us talking if I kept my voice at a normal level, and between the ovens and fans and the number of conversations going on in here to begin with, I figured no one would try eavesdropping. "I have a meeting with the board this afternoon."

Juan paused his chewing for a second and I saw the flash of recognition. It was every doctor's worst nightmare—a mistake on the job that might cost them their career. I didn't believe the mistake was mine, but I had to walk through this process anyway. If a patient sued the hospital, they wouldn't take it lying down. They'd get to the bottom of it and find out who did what, and that person would get the hammer.

"Ah..." His grunt of solidarity was about as much comfort as a wet blanket on a cold day, but I didn't really think there was anything anyone could even say to help take this weight off. The board was on a witch hunt and I was the first target because it was my operating table.

"Yeah, so the patient didn't die, but he might sue anyway. I still think the mistake was clerical, but there isn't any way to prove that without seeing all of his records before and after, which were of course immediately sealed and moved off the servers." I wished I'd done a better job going over his case more thoroughly, but I hadn't. Not only was it an emergency situation, but his previous doctors hadn't forwarded the charts over to us until an hour before my first incision.

This was the perfect sort of case to push for uniform health organization. It made so much more sense to organize patient files in a singular central database the way other countries did it. Americans deserved to have all their data at their doctor's fingertips the instant they walked through any practice's front door. It would possibly have saved this entire situation.

"Well, all you can do is take your lumps, man. The truth is like a lion..." Juan was always saying things like that... Things I didn't quite understand that he eventually spelled out for me. He looked me in the eye as I raised my eyebrows, and I didn't even have to ask him to explain. "You don't have to tell someone when a lion walks into the room. The truth will come out, and everyone will see it. So just sit tight and ride the waves."

Now that was an idiom I understood completely. Except, this wasn't a calm ocean and I wasn't on a surfboard. I was on the edge of what I believed would be a tempest, and looking into the storm wall had me shitting my pants.

"Thanks..." I looked down at my plate and felt a little less hungry after talking about that, but I continued to eat. Silence fell over the table, but the din of silverware clinking on plates and the chatter of happy voices surrounded us. My food was almost gone when I looked up at the vending machines not ten yards away and saw the shapely form of the gorgeous woman from the parking garage last week.

A smile crept over my face as I checked her out, and I wasn't shy about staring. Her back was to me. She wore green scrubs today, form fitting. They hugged her ass and showed a faint outline of her panties underneath, and I felt the same stirring inside my gut as I watched her bend to take her soda out of the collection tray.

Juan whistled under his breath and it caught my attention. I glanced at him to see him nodding and grinning. "Yes... I agree."

My chuckle vibrated my chest, loosening me up. It was the lightest I'd felt all day, and I wasn't sure how to feel about that. If Kate were here, would I have felt this way? And was it cheating even if she'd been gone this long? My heart felt like it might be, but my dick twitched and craved something I'd been lacking for too long.

"Yeah, but she's really young. Probably just fresh out of college." I cringed at Juan's comment and looked away.

Twenty years was a huge age difference, though I doubted she was genuinely straight out of college. Besides, age was just a number after twenty-one, right?

My eyes snuck back up to where she was just standing, but she was gone. I briefly felt a tinge of disappointment, but it vanished and turned to frustration when a board member walked up to get his soda. The yo-yo was exhausting, but at least the high point was refreshing. I wasn't sure if Juan was right, but I didn't figure it mattered. There was no way she'd look my way twice. I was old and probably out of touch to her generation. And with the idea of a scandal looming, it was probably a good idea for me to not even try.

4

ROSE

After getting my soda from the vending machine, I went to the counter and got a ham and Swiss on rye. The day was pretty average. My routine was solidifying, and I felt good about working here. I walked past a table where I recognized a few of the nurses' faces but avoided eye contact. I didn't want them to invite me to sit with them—not because I didn't like them, but because I had no time for socialization and hanging out with coworkers could get messy.

I wanted a seat by myself where I could enjoy my sandwich and drink and scroll my phone in peace. As an introvert, having time to myself meant recharging after dealing with forced patient interaction for hours. I soaked up every second of silence and solitude that I could.

In fact, I took out my phone and eyed a table at the back of the room, then buried my nose in my phone screen as I walked that direction. I was so engrossed in my social feed that I didn't see where I was going and clumsily bumped into someone.

I gasped and jerked my head up to see it was the handsome doctor from the parking garage. He looked as shocked as I was at the collision, and I felt my cheeks get hot instantly. I couldn't stop smiling as I looked up at him, and his grin matched mine. I saw the empty tray in his hand and realized he was headed for the bussing station.

"I'm sorry," I said, and I took a step backward, but I couldn't look away. His blue eyes were so crystal clear and locked on me.

"It was my fault. I wasn't watching where I was going." He nodded at his tray. "Just finishing lunch..."

I waved my sandwich in the air as I slid my phone into my pocket. "I'm just sitting down to eat. I, uh..." I felt my throat swell as anxiety rose and the butterflies took over. The grin on Alana's face when she joked about him jumping my bones flashed through my head, only making my cheeks hotter, and I licked my lips.

"Mind if I join you?" he asked, and I felt like I couldn't speak.

I nodded and stepped aside for him to walk toward the trash cans. When he returned to my side, we walked to the only empty table in the cafeteria way in the back near the vending machines. I sat down and placed my sandwich and drink in front of me, and he sat down too, leaving one chair between us.

"How's your car? Everything running well?" Of course he would ask about my car. That was the entire reason we had met.

"Uh, yeah, it's good. Just left my charging wire plugged in that day..." My fingers shook as I folded open my sandwich, and I knew there was no way I was going to eat this in front of him.

"Good. I'm happy to help. I'm glad I passed through when you were in need." He seemed to relax a little, and I felt a bit flushed.

I wasn't sure what to say next. As such an introvert, I wasn't good at small talk or interacting with people on a social basis. It always left me feeling too self-conscious and vulnerable, so I avoided it at all costs. In my attempt to make this less awkward for myself, I reached for my soda and cracked it open and Dr. Hastings took the initiative to keep the conversation going.

"So, how long have you been working here again? I remember you said something..." His arm draped across the table, and I watched his bicep flex under his scrub top. It made my body warm as I imagined a chiseled physique under all that clothing.

"Uh, well, two weeks. I mean, this is three weeks now. Sorry." I winced, feeling stupid for that mistake. I was so flustered around him.

"Are you settling in and making friends? I could show you around, maybe, introduce you to some people." His offer was so kind, but the one thing I never did was mix work with pleasure. One little tiff outside of work based on someone's bad attitude would leave me in the lurch during work hours when adults got petty. No thanks.

"Uh, yeah, I've met most of my coworkers and I'm good with that. I don't really socialize with people I work with." My words flowed out of my mouth, and I watched a hint of some sort of negative emotion flash across his face before he flashed me a smile.

"Well, that's alright."

"It's just that socializing with people you work with gets messy." I was blurting stupid comments out now. I hated myself for that.

"I understand," he said, just as his phone chimed. I realized I probably sounded like a total jerk.

His eyes were on his phone screen and I felt horrible. He probably thought I meant him too, which I wasn't sure what I meant.

"I mean... Yes, that would be nice. I'm sorry..." My rambling and backpedaling probably sounded like floundering to him, and he raised his eyes to meet mine.

"I have to run. I have a patient. I'll catch you later?" he said as a question as he stood, and I nodded.

Dr. Cole Hastings walked away with a pep in his step, and my God, his ass was perfect. But I wasn't. I was an idiot and might have blown my chance.

5

COLE

My feet pounded the treadmill as I pushed myself. My six a.m. workout routine was almost bordering on a religious tradition. I wasn't a religious man, but I did treat my body like a temple as much as I could. I knew old age crept up too quickly on most folks and they never got ahead of the curve. I wanted to stay as youthful as I could for as long as I could.

The harder I pushed myself, the better it felt. But I couldn't outrun the stress of the pending litigation. Even the news on the television here at the gym was talking about it now. It appeared they were keeping my name out of things for the time being, but Twin Peaks was taking a beating in the press. The patient who had almost died was very vocal about healthcare reform. I couldn't fault him. I, myself, wanted it.

I tried to ignore the broadcast, but it was quite loud. Everyone in the gym had their eyes on a television somewhere in the room, and I had to stare down at the treadmill's screen to focus on something else. I thought of work and how I'd feel when I got there. I ran harder until I was panting and thought of ways to pleasantly distract myself at work too. The stress there was really getting to me.

Then I thought of the cute nurse I met, Rose—I didn't get her last name yet. The way we bumped into each other at lunch last week didn't feel like a coincidence. It felt like the universe was telling me that there was something there. Yes, she was new, but how often was it that you bumped into someone twice so casually?

Just thinking of her got me excited to get to work instead of dreading it. I'd have said she was my lucky charm, but after having asked her to do a tour with me and receiving her rejection in such an obvious manner, I realized nothing would ever come of it with her. But the freedom of knowing a woman could spark my soul the way Kate had gave me hope for the future. If not Rose, then someone else for sure. I finally felt ready to move on and start over, and I had Rose to thank for that. It wasn't a small thing.

I pressed the stop button and the treadmill slowed. Without even looking back up at the offending news broadcast, I slipped out of the gym and into the locker room. I showered and shaved, then dressed and packed my things up. I stopped by a coffee shop on my way to the hospital, and when I got there, I found a parking spot near the front row. I felt like my day was already looking up.

My team greeted me with a few updates on patients, and then I looked at my surgery roster to find out what my day looked like. With nothing on the schedule this morning, I took to rounds early. I carried my coffee with me and my tablet and stopped by my patients' rooms.

After my third, but definitely not least significant, patient, I had to use the toilet. Too much coffee meant frequent bathroom breaks in the morning. I was rounding the corner to head up the hall to the bathrooms when I smacked into someone walking the opposite way. I dropped my tablet, spilled my coffee, and cussed so loudly I thought the whole floor could hear. Worst of all, the poor nurse took a spill at my expense, landing only inches from the puddle of tepid brew.

"God, I'm sorry," I grunted, swiping at the few droplets of coffee on my scrub pants. When I looked down at her, I felt my chest constrict like a vacuum. "Rose?"

She chuckled and pushed herself up off the floor, and I felt like a fool. "Wow, if you're going to keep running into me, I'm going to need to start wearing a helmet." She stooped to pick up my tablet and handed it to me.

"God, I'm so sorry. I wasn't watching where I was going. I was in a hurry." Thankfully, the tablet was pretty sturdy. It wasn't cracked or chipped. I tucked it under my arm and sighed.

"It's alright. I'm on break and I just stopped to use the toilet." Her thumb pointed over her shoulder right where I was headed, and she crossed her arms over her middle. "I should, uh... I'll get janitorial to clean this up before someone slips."

"Hey, I can do that..." I glanced around and noticed one of the techs pushing a mop bucket this direction. It was time to mop, anyway. I just gave them the starting point. When I turned back to Rose, she was smiling at me and she hadn't left. I thought back to my invitation to show her around and how she resisted, then doubled back with an apology.

"I guess fate has it ordained that we should keep running into each other—literally." She laughed a little and snorted, which made me chuckle.

"I thought the same thing... Maybe I really am supposed to show you around and give you a tour." I tilted my head, and she seemed pleased by the idea.

"Yeah, sure. I have time to kill. Why not?" Rose stepped aside when the tech walked up. "Sorry about this," she told him, and I felt bad for making the mess.

"Just let me empty my bladder and we'll be set." I left her to watch the floor be mopped and went to the bathroom. After washing my hands, I came back and found her standing in almost the same spot.

She joined me and I began the tour. I took her through every wing of the hospital, including administrative. She asked lots of questions, and I introduced her to a few other nurses and doctors along the way, and when we were running out of time for her break, we headed back toward her hall.

"So you know a lot about Twin Peaks and the staff?" She had her hands in her scrubs pockets as she walked next to me, smiling up at me. She really was stunning, a piece of art. Her beautiful smile was offset by dimples, and the crop of freckles across the ridge of her nose was so faint I almost missed them, but I liked them.

"Yeah, well I've been around for a while. I just know it's rough getting settled in a new place, and I wanted to show you the ropes, help you make a few friends." Passing this off as my being friendly was the best way to test the waters. If she wasn't interested in anything, it was the best way to be able to back out without making her feel bad.

"I appreciate that... Honestly, though, having personal relationships with coworkers is sort of the bane of my existence. At the last place I worked, it just led to so much drama. Friends end up backstabbing, and I'm just not interested. I'm more of an introvert in that. I want to keep my personal life private. People at work knowing my stuff just doesn't sound good."

I listened and tried to read between the lines. It wasn't that she was averse to workplace relationships, more so that she'd been burned. "So you'd never consider a relationship with a coworker?" I asked, just hinting around. I tried to make it sound like a friendship with a mutual, but the smile on her lips when she answered made my chest swell a little.

"I guess it would depend on the person and the type of relationship."

I was really beginning to enjoy talking with Rose, and this was the third time we'd just randomly connected. It couldn't be a coincidence. Not to mention neither of us enjoyed our personal lives being talked about at work. I was sure that was something I had in common with a lot of people, but having it in common with her felt like something important.

"Well, here I am," she said, gesturing at the fourth floor nurses' station.

I wanted to ask her to coffee or something, but my tongue froze. I thought of Kate and how she'd feel. I thought of moving on and what it would mean and how I did feel ready, but I was still not so optimistic. Then I thought of the scandal and wondered what Rose would think of me if she knew I was that doctor. And before I was able to put a sentence together, she reached her hand out for a handshake.

"Thank you, Dr. Hastings, for the welcome tour three weeks late." She snickered and shook my hand, and I nodded.

"That's Cole, and you're welcome. Hopefully, we'll bump into each other again soon." I didn't mean it to be a pun, but she laughed and snorted again. It was the cutest thing in the world. I loved it.

"Just let me invest in a helmet first, maybe some knee pads too." She snorted again, and I found myself laughing with her.

"Well, hurry up. It could be tomorrow." I backed away, wishing I'd have had the guts to actually ask her out, but my mind, while seeming ready to move on, needed a bit more time to process things. Maybe next time I saw her would be the right time.

6

_____

ROSE

My feet slapped the concrete as I ran along the winding paths through the park. It was a beautiful day, though a tad on the warm side for me this morning. I wore a pair of spandex shorts and a tank top. My hair was tied up into a ponytail and I had my earbuds in, listening to music.

I was regretting my choice of music as the beat picked up and I found myself running faster than I wanted. Sighing, I took out my earbuds and slowed down my pace. At this rate, I wouldn't have the energy to do yoga, let alone clean later. My thoughts drifted to what I needed to get done tomorrow—grocery shopping, clean the apartment, laundry, call Mom, yoga with Alana.

I mentally added to my list as I ran past a couple walking their dog. They smiled and waved at me, and I gave them a small smile and continued on my way. I had a feeling my day tomorrow was going to be just as packed as every other weekend. The only difference was that I had something keeping me inwardly motivated. Monday's didn't seem so bad anymore.

After bumping into Dr. Hastings a few more times, I was starting to enjoy his presence. It made Friday seem a little depressing. If I was at work, there was at least a chance I'd bump into him. But weekends meant being away from the hospital and the only place I was guaranteed to have a chance.

I sighed as I came to a stop near a bench. I sat down, catching my breath. I took my phone out of the armband strapped around my bicep and checked the time. It was 9:30 already? Almost an hour had passed since I left my apartment, but it had felt like only minutes. My stamina was really increasing, and my goal of running a half-marathon in the fall was coming into view.

With a smile, I stood back up and started my cool down stretches. My body was glowing with sweat as I stood up, my hair sticking to my forehead and my cheeks flushed with exertion. I stretched my arms and legs, feeling the muscles loosen and relax. My skin was hot and damp, a slight breeze causing goosebumps to raise on my arms.

I was almost finished stretching when something bumped into me, and I turned around to see a basketball rolling away. My first instinct was to look up and glance around. I saw the basketball courts and knew that was where the ball had come from, but the handsome, smiling man jogging up to me didn't register until I saw those dazzling baby blues.

"Uh, Dr. Hastings?" I mumbled as I bent to retrieve the ball. He was sweaty, chest glistening in the sun from perspiration, and the sight made my breath catch. He was stunning—corded abs, muscular, well-defined chest and abs, and that five-o'clock shadow made my mouth water.

"Oh, hey, Rose..." He held his hands out as if waiting for me to throw him the ball. He stood a few yards away, and I froze like a deer in headlights. At least we hadn't physically collided this time, but his ball had hit me.

"Uh, sorry," I muttered, and I tried to toss him the ball, but I had zero hand-eye coordination and the ball bounced short of where he stood. He winked at me and bent to pick it up, then turned and jogged back to the court.

Before bumping into him, my plan had been to go home and do my yoga, but seeing him here made me feel giddy. I stood there watching him play basketball with another doctor I recognized from work. Then my legs started to get tired from the long run, so I sat on the bench.

I couldn't take my eyes off Dr. Hastings as he played basketball with his colleague. His athletic abilities and toned physique were mesmerizing to watch. The sight of him making a perfect shot and doing a little victory dance for me made my heart flutter.

I sat on the bench, trying to catch my breath from the run and also trying not to appear too obvious in my staring. But every time he looked over at me, I felt my cheeks flush with embarrassment. He was too good-looking for his own good, and it wasn't fair that he had to be so nice on top of it all.

I had to remind myself that he was a coworker and nothing would ever happen between us. I also reminded myself of how sticky relationships could be and how Alana would only lecture me about jeopardizing my employment status, which she relied upon. I had to pay my share of the rent, and that would be impossible if I didn't have a job because I messed around at work and got caught and fired.

So when he stole glances at me and winked a few times, I thought about getting up and leaving. Allowing myself to indulge in the eye candy was one thing, but knowing he was flirting with me while getting his workout in was another. He had already seemed a little too interested, though I had to admit I liked it. Still, workplace romances never worked out.

The ball bounced off the court again in my direction, and his friend was the one who retrieved it this time. He smiled at me and I nodded at him, but he wasn't nearly as good-looking as Dr. Hastings was. And while I should've gotten up and gone home, I was just enjoying watching them play too much to move.

But when their game ended and they slapped hands high in the air, I felt a bit of nervous flutters in my chest. I really wanted him to come talk to me, and simultaneously, I wanted to melt into the bench and vanish as if I hadn't been staring at him for over fifteen minutes. I had it bad for him, and it had to be obvious.

7

COLE

With each dribble of the basketball, I felt more alive than ever before. Juan's eyes on me, burning with intensity, fueled my every move. I could feel the sweat trickling down my brow as we continued our heated game of one-on-one. The sun beat down relentlessly, but I didn't care. All that mattered was the ball in my hands and the audience of one who couldn't seem to tear her gaze away from me.

Rose sat on the bench watching, and I felt her eyes on me the entire time. The random chance that we'd bump into each other again made it one hundred percent obvious to me that something was brewing between us. I didn't think for a second that she had tracked me down. I believed in fate, however, and the stars were aligning between us.

I spun around him, feinting a layup before pulling back and sinking a three-pointer. "Game point," I panted, chest heaving with exertion but adrenaline coursing through my veins. Juan's jaw set in determination as he took the ball, dribbling it up the court. I knew I had to bring my A-game if I wanted to walk away with the win.

I readied myself on defense, mirroring his every move as he weaved his way down the court. With only a few seconds left on the imaginary clock, Juan double-pumped, trying to fake me out. I didn't bite, staying grounded and reaching up to swat the ball away at the last second. The ball sailed through the air and landed in Rose's lap, who deftly caught it with a grin.

"Well, looks like I win," I said, wiping the sweat from my brow as I strolled over to claim my prize, a punch to Juan's shoulder. "Rematch?" Juan asked, extending a hand for a good-natured handshake.

"Maybe next time," I replied before turning my attention back to Rose. She was still there, still staring, and now she held my ball in her hands as if she was waiting for me to come retrieve it. I pulled my eyes off Rose as I followed Juan to the bench where our gym bags and water bottles were stashed. He was heaving for air and I was pretending I wasn't winded.

"So, you gonna ask her out or what?" he panted, shoving a water bottle into my chest. I caught it and took a long swig of the cold, refreshing liquid before responding.

"I don't know, man," I said, feigning indifference even though my heart was racing. "It's been a while since I've done this whole dating thing." I didn't mention that Rose was the first person to catch my attention in quite some time, not since before the accident that had changed my life forever.

Juan gave me a knowing look as he pulled a towel from his bag and wiped the sweat from his brow. "You're stalling, man. Just go talk to her already. Worst-case scenario, she shoots you down and you're no worse off than you are now."

I glanced over at Rose, who was still watching us intently, a coy smile on her lips as she bounced the basketball between her legs. I took a deep breath, trying to steady my nerves. Juan was right. I had nothing to lose—except my heart. That was still an irrational fear I had, that any woman I allowed to get close to me in the future would be ripped away from me the way Kate was. Then I thought of the obvious age difference and why a woman Rose's age would ever want to date a man my age seriously when she could have someone closer to her age who would be around much longer than me.

"Yeah, I just don't know," I told him, but I couldn't shake the idea that fate had sent Rose to me, or maybe Kate had.

"I can't keep up with the silver fox, I guess. I gotta bolt, man. I'll catch ya Monday." Juan gave me one of his odd hand-slap, fist-bump hand-shakes, and I nodded at him.

"Later," I called as he shouldered his bag and walked off. Then I chuckled at his nickname for me and ran a hand through my sweat-soaked hair. I picked up my own bag and hung it from my shoulder, then started walking over toward where Rose sat. She held my ball under her arm and stood up, smirking at me as I stopped in front of her.

"Good game," she said, tossing me the ball a little more accurately this time. I caught it and tucked it between my elbow and hip and grinned at her.

"I have a fan?" I noticed her eyes sweep down over my sweaty skin and then back up to my face. She couldn't hide the attraction. I saw it in her eyes.

"You're no Michael Jordan, but you kept me entertained." Rose tucked her phone into an arm band strapped to her right bicep, and I took the moment to admire that she, too, was a bit sweaty. I'd seen her run up and start stretching, though I hadn't known it was her until Jordan lost control of the ball and I had to chase it over here the first time.

"Out for a run?" I asked, noticing her sneakers. She was in great shape, and those Spandex looked amazing on her. It was so different seeing her curves in something form fitting instead of loose scrubs.

"Uh, yeah… I'm training to run a half-marathon in the fall." She tucked a stray wisp of hair around her ear and smiled at me. "You're pretty good at basketball. Did you play in college?" She batted her eyelashes at me and her eyes moved downward again. It was like she couldn't stop admiring my body. I took care of myself and made sure to keep in good shape.

"No, actually. I played a little in high school, but my passion in college was just medicine." And Kate… but I wasn't going to bring that up now. Not when we were finally forming a real rapport. "Hey, would you like to go across the street to that new smoothie shop and get a protein shake?" I raised my eyebrows and her smile brightened.

"I'd love to." She shrugged both shoulders slightly and fell into step next to me.

We walked across the street, and I pulled my wallet out and paid for two banana protein shakes, and we sat on a bench in the shade watching cars pass between us and the park. I watched her lips wrap around the straw and the shake ascend into her mouth, and she smiled.

"It's so good." Her face lit up, and I grinned.

"I knew you'd love it. I come here almost every Saturday from April to September. Juan and I play basketball or go for a run. Sometimes, we do a little cross fit too." I slurped my own smoothie as she nodded and swallowed a huge gulp.

"I've only been around a short time, but this park is my favorite. I have to commute all the way across town, but it's worth it. None of the other parks have trails like these for running." She sighed happily. "How long have you lived in Denver?"

"Oh, gosh, I grew up here. I'm ancient," I joked, and she snickered.

"Is that why Juan called you the silver fox?" A smirk played on her lips and she continued. "Or was that nickname given to you by other women for your good looks?" Rose was a natural at this, and it made me feel a little inadequate. I was so far out of this dating game, I didn't even know how people today flirted with each other. She was clearly dominating this conversation too, which I didn't mind.

"I suppose it could be either." I sucked on my straw and realized my obvious failure to drop a hint. So while she enjoyed a sip of her smoothie, I continued. "I mean, Juan calls me that because I told him I found you attractive, so he thinks something's going on."

A noticeable blush crept across her cheeks and she looked down at her cup. The pink tinted drink swirled around inside it as she tipped it back and forth, and I enjoyed the bit of embarrassment that hedged her in. Then she looked up and met my gaze with a serious expression so bold I felt taken off guard.

"You find me attractive?" Her tongue drew along her bottom lip, and I watched it. I wondered what the smoothie would taste like right off her lip.

"I thought that was obvious, and I'm sorry if it wasn't... Uh, would you like to have dinner with me sometime?"

I really put myself out there shooting my shot like this. I didn't know if she was even that interested in me. Watching me play basketball without my shirt on and joining me for a smoothie didn't mean she wanted to date me.

"Uh, well, we work together..." Her words lingered between us, and I remembered her saying something about relationships with coworkers getting messy, which I understood. But we weren't exactly working side by side.

"This is because of your not wanting to associate with coworkers off the clock?" If it never worked out, it wouldn't be that hard to avoid each other at the hospital.

"Actually, no. I thought there was a no-fraternization policy at work?" She narrowed her eyes at me and sucked on her straw, and I bobbed one shoulder.

35

"I don't think it matters that much if we're not in the same department, but I get it. I'm not worried, but I understand if you're too uncomfortable." The wind was slowly fading from my sails, but her head shaking put a pause in that deflation.

"Alright, well, no. If you're not worried, I'm not worried. Just tell me when and where. I'd love to have dinner."

Rose beamed at me again, and finally, after weeks of back and forth, I had scored a date with her. I was interested to see where this went, even if it went nowhere. It'd been so long since I'd been on a date that I forgot what it felt like. It was a good feeling, and I hoped it lasted a while.

8

ROSE

I stood in front of the mirror Monday morning brushing my teeth as Alana walked in with her makeup bag. She'd been gone all weekend, which I'd forgotten about when I went out for my run Saturday morning. I came back to an empty apartment and remembered about her trip to see her mother for the weekend. She got in after I went to bed last night, and I hadn't even gotten a chance to tell her about what happened at the park.

"Morning," she grumbled as she plopped her bag on the bathroom counter. We always hot-swapped the bathroom because I had to be at work by eight and she woke at a quarter 'til to get ready for her own job.

"Good morning," I said cheerfully as I spat the toothpaste out of my mouth into the sink and turned the water on.

Alana reached for a towel in the cupboard behind me and set it on the top of the toilet before turning on the shower water. Then she looked back at me and said, "You are too happy for this time of day."

I chuckled at her as I rinsed my toothbrush then got a drink of water to rinse my mouth. "Maybe that's because I have a date coming up..." I grinned like an idiot and tapped the water out of my toothbrush on the edge of the sink.

"Shut up, no way." Her mood changed a little, but she still looked grumpy and tired. "Who? When?"

I put my toothbrush into the ceramic holder and leaned on the counter facing her. She crossed her arms over her chest and waited for me to answer.

"Remember that cute doctor I told you about who jumped my car?" I remembered her words of warning about working with someone I was dating, but I had pushed those thoughts away. If Cole wasn't worried about it, why should I?

"Wait. He asked you out? When? You didn't say anything to me on Friday." Alana yawned, and I caught a whiff of her morning breath and cringed.

"I was out for a run at the park Saturday morning when you left, and I bumped into him." I snickered at how that seemed to be our habit. I'd run into that man more times than was humanly possible. "And let me tell you, he is really frickin' hot when he's shirtless." I wagged my eyebrows and she shook her head at me. Her hair stuck up at odd angles and there was a rat's nest in the back. It looked like she hadn't slept well.

"Well, just be careful. Like I said, dating a coworker gets messy, hon. You don't want to shoot yourself in the foot when you just got the job." She didn't look enthused by my excitement, but I wasn't going to let her get me down.

"I'll be fine. We're in different departments, anyway." I backed up a few steps and grabbed the doorknob. "Oh, and I used all the hot water," I confessed and winced as I pulled the door shut after me, and she groaned loudly.

Snickering, I made my way to the front door where I used my phone to check the temperature outside. I opted for no jacket this morning and took my keys and wallet and headed out. The sun was warm this morning, and I thought about walking to work, but I knew how tired I'd be by the time I got off, so I climbed into my car and drove there.

When I walked onto the floor, a few other nurses were huddled around the nurses' station talking. Typically, I'd have avoided anything to do with that clusterfuck, but this morning, I was in a really good mood and hoping to bump into Dr. Hastings. I meandered over to the group of Chatty Cathys in the hopes one of them might have seen him and could tell me where to "bump" into him again.

One of the nurses Cole had introduced me to was standing with them, so I smiled at her and she waved me over. "Hey, Rose, nice to see you again."

"Hey, Kiki, good morning. Have you seen Dr. Hastings this morning?" I wanted to keep it super casual. I didn't want any of them knowing there was something potentially going on between us for a lot of reasons, but mainly, I didn't want HR finding out and I hated gossip. Especially when it was about me.

"No, I haven't, but man, I'd like to." She snickered at me, and the other nurses mumbled their agreement as I grinned.

"I see Dr. Silver Fox has caught a few eyes?" I joked, and instantly, the women all brightened up and looked at me.

"That's a catchy nickname. Dr. Foxy..." Kiki laughed and fanned herself. "He's hot though, right? Every single lady here knows it. And girl, have you seen him without a shirt?" Her hand swept up and down past her face as if she were on a beach sweating. If anyone could give me a better read on what Cole Hastings was really like, it was the people he worked with. But getting information out of them would be tricky if I didn't want to let on that something was brewing between us.

"I can't say that I have," I told them, lying. That man was chiseled more perfectly than Zeus, and just thinking of his sweat-slicked body made me feel a few degrees warmer.

"Well, don't get your hopes up," another nurse said. Her nametag read *Jenn*, and I turned my attention on her. "He's a grump, won't even flirt a little. Too professional." Jenn was a bit older than me, but she had a ring on her finger. What was she even doing flirting with a single man when she was married? No wonder Dr. Hastings wouldn't flirt with her.

"Oh, Jenn, you know that's not true." Kiki shook her head and looked back at me, leaning in as if she were going to share a dirty secret or something. I hated this. I wanted to know where he was, not all the gossip. This was why friendships with coworkers were just not a good idea. "He's just mourning."

My eyebrows rose and I said, "What?"

"Yeah, his wife died in a bad car accident a few years back and he's never been the same. We like to flirt with him and stuff, but I think he's just heartbroken. No woman has ever gotten him to open up. Not likely to happen until he's ready to move on. He hasn't dated anyone that I know of since it happened. But hey, we can enjoy the eye candy, if you know what I mean." Kiki winked at me, and I had to force a smile.

Of all the information I could have discovered this morning about Cole Hastings, this wasn't even on my radar. "I know what you mean," I told her absently, but I backed away with the new revelation in mind. Learning that Dr. Hastings' wife was dead helped answer a lot of questions I had.

It made sense now why he was that good-looking but still single. Why a wealthy, handsome doctor hadn't settled down well into his forties. Because he had. He'd been married and now he was a widower, and if what Kiki said was true, I was the one helping break that curse. I didn't know if that was a good thing or a bad thing because if he was still mourning, I might have to compete with the memory of his dead wife. It didn't put me off the idea of going to dinner, but it did help me see what I was getting into more clearly.

I used a computer to sign into my shift and looked over my first few patients' charts and what I had to do, but the entire time, I was thinking of dinner with Dr. Silver Fox. Kiki said he hadn't opened up to anyone and I wondered what that meant. He probably had walls so high around his heart, it was impossible to get to the real him, but if anyone could help him lower those walls, I knew I could.

And the fact that he had asked me to dinner—on a date—meant he was probably feeling ready to move on. It was a good sign but one I wasn't going to put too much stock in until we actually went to dinner. I was really glad I spoke to the nurses this morning. I felt like it prepared me more for what was to come, and that made me even more eager to find out when and where he'd want to eat dinner.

Dr. Cole Hastings, the silver fox of Twin Peaks, was a mystery I couldn't wait to solve.

COLE

ose looked stunning in the simple black gown she wore. She had her hair tied up into a knot on her head and she wore light makeup. I opened the passenger car door, and she got in and buckled herself in as I shut it after her. I was a bundle of nerves. Dating was easy when I was eighteen or twenty years old. Now in my forties, I felt like I'd been out of the game for so long I didn't know what I was doing.

I had agonized all week about where to take her. When we exchanged numbers on Monday afternoon, she mentioned that her favorite food was Italian, but I knew pasta was a bit messy and I didn't want her to feel awkward eating and wiping her mouth every few minutes. I ended up choosing an Italian place anyway, though, and now, Friday night, I was here picking her up.

I climbed into the driver's seat, feeling out of place, and started the car. She sat quietly with her clutch on her lap. Her fingers tapped her knees and the radio hummed in the background. I didn't know how I'd gone from a suave, charming man to this awkward bundle of energy, but I had. I didn't even know how to break the ice.

So she did it.

"You look nice tonight." Rose's compliment made me feel like a buffoon. Of course I thought she looked gorgeous, so why hadn't I said that?

"Uh, thank you... I wasn't sure what to wear. It's been a long time since..." I felt foolish for even thinking of Kate or my past, or dating.

"It's okay. I think you picked a nice suit." Rose's warm smile put me at ease, and I appreciated how she was trying to make me feel comfortable. As a woman in her late twenties, she probably went on dates all the time. This stuff was simple for her, and I was struggling.

"You look nice too, Rose, and I'm sorry if I seem out of place or uncomfortable." Bringing up my dead wife on the first date didn't seem like good etiquette, so I said nothing, but I felt the weight of it. It was like Kate's ghost was hovering tonight and I didn't know if that was good or bad, if I should be doing this, or if she'd be upset by it.

"It's okay." Rose reached over and patted my knee. "Kiki told me..."

I glanced at her, and the knowing smile she had brought a tinge of sadness. Everyone at work knew about what happened with Kate. They'd all seen me fall apart and attempt to put myself back together. It was inevitable that someone would tell Rose anyway, so I couldn't be upset about that. I just wished I got to control that narrative.

But like everything else in life, I had control over very little. She would eventually find out about the surgery screw up and what I was going through with the board, and when she did that, it might taint her view of me, so for now, I just wanted to put anything negative aside and enjoy the night.

"If it's alright, I'd rather not talk about it."

"Totally fine. I'm here for the food, anyway," she joked and I smiled.

We fell into a natural banter about the Italian restaurant, and given she had only moved to Denver a few weeks ago, I felt good about being able to introduce her to something I knew she'd love.

We pulled into the parking lot about a quarter past seven and parked. I opened her door, and she got out and put her arm around mine. I led her inside with her fingers wrapped around my bicep, and I felt more comfortable already.

The host showed us to a private table near the back of the room and we settled in. I ordered spaghetti and Rose ordered lasagna, and we enjoyed the free breadsticks while we waited for our food.

"So, tell me a little more about yourself. Where do you see yourself in five years?" It'd been so long since I had a relationship with a woman, I didn't know where to start, but compatibility seemed like a smart step. If we had wildly different futures in mind, it wouldn't be smart to continue pursuing something no matter how gorgeous I thought she was.

"Honestly," she said, smiling, "maybe dating a hot doctor..." The smirk on her lips made me chuckle, and I grinned at her.

"That's fair... So, dating a hot doctor and what? Do you like Denver? Are you planning to stay here or do you have your eyes set somewhere else?" I liked her flirty attitude. It was definitely helping me relax a bit.

"I love Denver, and it's not just because of the hot doctors." She winked at me and continued, "I've always wanted to live here. I grew up in a tiny little village with nothing. I always wanted to be a city girl, but until my mom is no longer with us, I can't move very far. I'd like to travel and see the world, but once I'm settled here, I don't think I'll move away." Rose dipped her breadstick in a cup of marinara and took a bite, and I was already feeling better about this.

"Denver's my home, born and raised. I'll never move away, but I, too, like the idea of traveling. I figure when I retire—hopefully early—I'll have enough energy to see the world. I can't think of anything better to do with my golden years." I smiled at her and picked up a bread-stick to munch on.

"Oh, gosh, yes. I mean, I don't necessarily want to wait until I'm old, but there are so many places I want to go. The pyramids, Greece, The Great Wall..." She had a dreamy look in her eye, and I tried not to cringe when she said the word "old". I hoped that wasn't how she thought of me. I knew my silver hair spoke volumes about my age, but I was by no means old yet.

"I'd love to see places stateside too. I want to go to New York and hear the Philharmonic play. I have a few of their recordings on vinyl." I was really warming up to her, and when she smiled at my comment, I noticed a dimple I hadn't seen. She was so beautiful it was distracting.

"Oh, you like the symphony too? I swear I could sit and listen to symphonic music all day. It's so relaxing and calming. I wasn't really into orchestra when I was in high school, but I wish my mom had been well off enough to afford lessons for me. I would've loved to learn to play violin." Rose smiled and tilted her head. "It seems like we have a lot in common."

"It does..." I looked up at her and took a deep, relaxing breath. This wasn't as awkward or difficult as I imagined it would be, but maybe that was the company. Rose was putting me at ease, and I appreciated that she and I were clicking so easily.

"What about your hobbies?" I asked, and she snickered.

"Is this Twenty Questions?" Her eyebrows tented in the center, and she popped the last bite of a breadstick into her mouth.

"I'm sorry. I told you it's been a while."

"That's okay... Uh, hobbies... I'm a runner, so I do that a lot. I love coffee shops too, so if you know any great cafés with decent atmosphere, tell me, please. And oh, I love baking. If you stick around me very long, you'll have to up your workout routine or you'll gain a few pounds."

Things were going so smoothly we didn't even notice when dinner hadn't arrived until forty minutes later. As we ate, we chatted about work and how things were going at the hospital. The topic of the hospital updating their policies and changing reporting procedures came up, and I got tense for a while. I was thankful for the waiter distracting us by offering more breadsticks and drinks, and I changed the subject almost immediately.

"So, I was thinking we could go for a drink after we're done eating, if you'd like."

Rose smiled softly and nodded, then she said, "Alright, but I get to pick the spot. My roommate told me about this place I want to check out, and I've been dying to go. She's just too busy. What do you think? Have you heard of the Déjà Vu club?" I'd heard of it and knew it well. The problem was it wasn't my scene at all. I was pushing the age limit for things like that, but her smile and the expression on her face were so hopeful. How could I tell her no?

"I have, and I know right where it is." So there were a few things about her that weren't a perfect match to me. I knew those things would shift and change over time, anyway. All in all, Rose and I got along so well that I knew the small differences wouldn't matter much, except maybe our age difference, and we still had time to discuss that. This was just the first date.

ROSE

The music was loud but the atmosphere was incredible. We walked into the club just after nine, and it was already packed with men and women drinking and dancing. The look on Cole's face showed a bit of apprehension, and as I looked around, I saw why. Everyone in this place was my age or younger. He probably felt a bit out of touch or uncomfortable, but I remembered what Kiki had said about his needing to open up, and I felt like this would bring him back to his dating years.

"Want a drink?" I shouted over the din of music, and his eyes flashed with a touch of desperation as he nodded. I chuckled as I took his hand and dragged him to the bar. It was a bit quieter on this side of the club, making it easier to hear the bartender and place our order. I got a sex on the beach and Cole ordered a light beer, which I rolled my eyes at.

When we had our drinks, we perched on barstools and sipped them as we adjusted to the mood. I faced him, and he sat with his knees outward, eyes scanning the gyrating club with its thumping melody and pulsing lights. He looked really out of place with his tie and stiff demeanor, and I wondered how I could get him to loosen up a little and have fun.

"So, did you used to go clubbing? I mean... when you were dating?" My question came out a bit more awkward than I planned, but Cole looked grateful for the distraction from his surroundings. Women were staring at him, and not in a good way. He was easily fifteen years older than most of the men in this place, but as such a hot silver fox, I felt like I was showing off what a score he was.

"Not really..." He smiled at me, but I could tell he wasn't comfortable here. "But this is okay." He brought his beer to his lips and drank deeply, and I decided it was time to do something bigger to help him relax.

I picked up my drink and downed it, then raised my glass to the bartender and held up two fingers. "Time to have some fun," I told Cole, and I slid off my stool. I wasn't exactly dressed for clubbing, but the little black dress I wore was at least easy to move in.

The music picked up, and I dipped and swayed right there, not even bothering to join those on the dance floor getting their groove on. I found a rhythm and put my entire body into it, and Cole ate it up. His eyes scanned up and down my body, making eye contact now and then, and when I turned my back to him, knowing his eyes were on my ass, I noticed a few women staring at me, so I danced even harder.

When the bartender brought our drinks, I handed one to Cole, who gave me a skeptical expression, and I smirked. "Just drink it. Loosen up a bit... let's have fun," I told him, but I leaned in really close to add, "You won't regret it." As I backed away, I noticed his Adam's apple bob up and down and felt a rush of attraction sweep down through my body, pooling in my core.

The liquor was already hitting me, making me a bit freer. My inhibitions were vanishing as I downed my second drink and returned to dancing for him. The song changed, changing my rhythm, but not my excitement. The more he stared at me, the riskier I got until I was touching him, petting his chest and playing with his tie. I loosened it and let it hang around his shoulders, then undid the top few buttons of his shirt.

When I let my hand slide down over his groin, I saw a twitch of hunger flit across his face and his hand wrapped around my wrist as he gently set my palm on his thigh. So he wasn't into public displays of affection, but I knew I was getting to him. Just one brush over his lap was enough to feel the bulge there. He was turned on.

So I turned it up again.

Cole finished his beer, and then downed the mixed drink, and I closed in on him. I let his knee slide between my thighs and I ground on his leg, moving my hips in a serpentine motion as I rested both hands on his shoulders. His hands curled around my hips and his eyes looked down at my chest where my dress had crept slightly lower, exposing more of my cleavage.

I was starting to get drunk, and that was making me horny too. I shut out everyone else in the room and focused on his expression, not breaking the eye contact I had going with Cole until he leaned forward and whispered into my ear, "What are you doing?"

I grinned and turned my head so I could speak right into his ear, then I licked his earlobe and bit down softly before I spoke. His growl of approval encouraged me so I said, "I'm helping you loosen up. What are you going to do about it?" My pelvis rode his thigh harder when he lifted his leg slightly, and I could tell I was getting wet. Coming to this club was an excellent idea.

"I think we should go," he said back to me, and at first I thought he sounded upset. I swallowed hard and backed away, but his hand kept me there, straddling his thigh. His eyes swept down over my body again and then landed on my lips. "Fuck," he whispered, but I couldn't hear him. All I could do was read his lips.

He wanted to go? Then we would go, and I didn't know where he planned to go but even if it was just his car, I hoped he had no intention of ending our night.

I backed away, and he reached into his wallet and dropped a few twenties on the bar to pay for our drinks. Then he stood and put his hand in the small of my back. I headed for the front door and he walked behind me. I was a little nervous, but his hand slid down over the curve of my ass and squeezed and it sent a thrill through me.

When his fingers found the hem of my skirt and he started inching it up, I glanced over my shoulder to see how close he was. No one was watching us. Cole's body was almost touching mine, and his fingers danced along the elastic lace of my panties.

We hit the sidewalk in a rush of adrenaline, and the chill of the air cooled my skin significantly. I turned and walked backward, and Cole closed in on me, hands gripping my hips. His lips crashed into mine, and I draped my arms over his shoulders as his body pressed against me. We continued moving along the side of the building in the darkness, and his hands groped every inch of my torso. When I finally came up for air, we were standing between two parked cars.

"Uh, so..." I breathed, desperate to kiss him again.

"My car," he grunted and continued pushing me farther into the darkness. There were more cars in the parking lot now, and fewer people. I let Cole herd me between the cars into the dark corner where he parked beneath a burnt-out streetlamp. He opened the back door, and I started to get in, but he pulled me back and climbed in first.

I grinned at him as I climbed in after him and shut the door, and my dress bunched up around my waist as I lifted a leg and straddled him. Just coming down on his lap made a chill go up my back, and an ache started low in my groin.

"You really want this?" he asked, his voice husky with lust. He didn't sound hesitant. He sounded delirious with desire for me, and I felt the same way.

"Fuck yes," I mumbled before crushing my mouth against his again. He was an animal, grabbing my body and pulling me down hard onto his lap. His cock was fully erect now, just waiting to be let out of those cotton slacks to have fun.

I wriggled around on his lap, trying to get comfortable. His hand slid beneath my skirt and underneath my panties, his digits delving inside me without any warning. I whimpered against his mouth at the sudden intrusion, but it felt so good.

His fingers were everywhere, touching and caressing, finding all the right spots. My hips began to gyrate against his touch and against his hardness that was still trapped between us. "Damn it," I moaned against his mouth. "I want you now." My core throbbed, aching for him to penetrate me. I knew the orgasm would be intense, and I couldn't get to it fast enough.

His hands traveled up my thighs and pushed my skirt higher up around my waist. Then he reached for his fly and unbuttoned his pants. I could hear the sound of his zipper being lowered in the darkness, and a rush of desperation made me whine. My fingers knotted in his hair, and I felt his hand moving between us, pulling his dick out.

"Shit…" I hissed when it brushed the inside of my thigh. I hadn't even gotten my panties off yet, but I wanted him inside me. The alcohol made my head spin and my chest pound, and I tried to rise up and shimmy the silky undergarments off, but Cole reached up and hooked a finger around the crotch and pulled them aside.

It made me hiss to feel him touch me again, and I lowered back down slightly. His cock slid across my entrance, revealing how much moisture I'd made. My pussy screamed to be touched too.

"God, Rose," Cole breathed, and I hovered there, on my knees just above his dick as I kissed him. Suddenly, I wanted this to last, to feel this chemistry and sizzle for as long as I could.

"You like this?" I asked him, biting his lower lip and rocking my hips so my pussy teased his head. It teased me too, slipping ever so gently through my moisture, taunting the bundle of nerves just inside my entrance that wanted to feel pleasure.

"I haven't felt this in decades," he growled, and he grabbed my hip and squeezed. His grip was hard and desperate. No doubt, it was intense for him if I was feeling it too.

"You want me to tease you?" I purred, kissing along his jawline to his ear. His cologne invaded my senses and I forgot any sense of decency.

"I think you've been doing that already." Cole's thumb reached up and pushed under my panties and rubbed my clit, and I bit my lip and whimpered. His touch drove me wild.

"Oh, my God, I'm so on fire," I whimpered. My need to feel his skin against mine was overwhelming, but I didn't want to strip completely off. The windows were fogged, but I was starting to get really drunk, and I had no idea how he felt, but between the wine at the restaurant and our few drinks here, both of us were probably feeling it.

"Yeah, I know… I want that pussy of yours down around my cock, but I don't want it to be over fast." He kissed me again, and I arched my neck up, letting him kiss down my neck to my breastbone. His lips peppered hot kisses along my skin, and I reached up and tugged the front of my dress down, exposing my right breast and nipple, which he greedily took into his mouth and nibbled on.

"Fuck," I grunted when he sucked and swirled on my nipple as he rubbed my clit with his thumb. "I don't want to wait anymore," I told him, and I rocked my hips harder. When I started to slowly descend over his dick, I groaned in pleasure. It was bigger than I expected him to be. "Oh, God," I moaned into the darkness as he filled me up. "Fuck, fuck, fuck, you feel so good."

Cole placed both hands on my ass and pulled me down harder onto him.

I gasped at the fullness and then leaned forward, resting my forearms on the back seat as he thrust up into me. My pussy was so tight and hot around him that every time he moved, it felt like he was stretching me more. It had been a while since I'd had sex with anyone, and Cole felt so good inside me, I didn't even care about the stretching pains.

"Fuck..." I moaned, grinding against him. "Oh, my God..."

His fingers dug into my hips and he pulled me in even closer, our bodies smashing together as we rocked together in the backseat. His breath was hot on my neck, his teeth nipping at my skin as we fucked each other in the dark.

"I need to come..." I whimpered, rocking harder against him. "Oh, my God, I'm going to come."

"Fuck, yes," he growled in my ear and sped up his thrusts.

Heat built between my legs, and I moaned louder as my orgasm exploded through my body like fireworks on the Fourth of July. My pussy clenched around his dick, and he groaned loudly against my chest. His teeth bit down on my nipple again, heightening the pleasure as I convulsed and spasmed. It was glorious and made me giddy.

The alcohol had fully taken effect now, and my eyes were heavy with relaxation and lust, and I claimed his lips again for another kiss. Cole's hunger continued while my body began to come down, and I started moving against him, finding the rhythm he set and grinding in time with his thrusts.

"Oh, fuck..." he groaned against my mouth. "I'm gonna..."

I bit his lower lip and rocked harder, grinding my hips into his as he came. His cock jerked inside me, spurting his load deep inside me, and he growled a low rumble that vibrated my chest.

"Wow..." he panted, collapsing back against the seat.

I collapsed against his chest, my panting mixing with his as our breaths came in ragged gasps. My dress was around my waist and my panties were still pushed to the side around him. Cole's dick was still inside me, and I felt him twitching, my muscles clenching around him.

"Damn," I finally managed to say, lifting my head and looking at him through heavy-lidded eyes. "That was…"

"Incredible," he finished for me, and he kissed me again. This time, it was sloppy and wet and messy, but I didn't care. I felt so dizzy and sleepy, and I wrapped my arms around his neck and rested my forehead on his shoulder.

His head reclined backward on the headrest and his arms pulled me against him. I never felt when he got soft or if he moved me off his lap. Before the waves of pleasure ceased, I had passed out, drunk on alcohol and sex, and totally at ease in his arms.

11

COLE

I sat outside the boardroom with my head resting on the wall behind me and my eyes closed. We'd just gone through a very intense meeting about the pending lawsuit aimed at the hospital, primarily, but they were looking for a scapegoat now. Corporate would rather tank my individual career than admit fault, and now they had a nurse willing to testify that she knew it was my mistake.

Anger didn't even begin to describe what I was feeling and I just wanted to escape. I thought of Friday night last weekend when Rose got a little drunk and did that lap dance for me. Everyone in that club was fifteen years younger than me and it made me feel a bit out of place, but when she started doing that, I was lost in her and nothing else mattered.

I lost a bit of control over myself too, getting carried away with the idea that she actually wanted me. We were both drunk and it led to incredible sex in my car, after which she passed out on my chest for a good thirty minutes before I felt sober enough to drive her home. She rattled off her address, and I walked her up to the front door. Her roommate didn't seem thrilled to see her coming home black-out drunk, but I was a perfect gentleman once I realized how drunk she was.

We'd spoken this week a few times too, and while things were slightly awkward given that we couldn't just come out and talk about the sex because we were at work, she gave no indication that she was upset with me. It was a mild relief to my heart that good things could coexist among the weeds in the garden that was my life.

"Dr. Hastings?" I heard a voice say, and I opened my eyes to see my HR rep standing next to me. I wasn't a fool. These HR people never looked out for the individual. They weren't employed by a third-party company designed to advocate for employees the way a union operated. They were employed by the hospital and its greater owners to advocate in the interest of what was best for the organization. It made me hate everything about working for such a large entity now that I was under the gun.

"Yeah," I said, and I scrubbed a hand over my face and rubbed my eyes. Then I looked over at her as she sat down in the seat next to me.

The blue pencil skirt she wore inched up above her knees as she placed her laptop on her lap and rested her hands on it. She'd been in the meeting with me and heard everything the hospital board was saying about this situation. I'd been forced to give testimony detailing the entire procedure down to trying to remember what we talked about or whether any jokes were told. I swore they paid off that nurse to say what she said, that I'd known about the patient's comorbidity and drug interactions. But none of that was on his chart until after the procedure was finished and he was in his recovery room.

"Dr. Hastings," she started, and she glanced around nervously, "I'm not here on official business from Premier Health." This was interesting. She looked nervous to be talking to me, and if she was nervous, it wasn't because I was a threat. It was because she was taking a risk.

"Then why are you here?" I was too grumpy to deal with drama or hearsay. Their throwing me under the bus was a load of shit. I didn't deserve to have my career tanked because someone in administration flaked on their responsibility and a patient was injured. The hospital didn't want the suit to come down on them, and they were finding ways to make it someone else's fault to distance them from the mistake that was clearly their responsibility to correct.

"I just wanted to tell you, I think what they're doing to you is a crock of shit." Her lips pursed and I watched her nostrils flare. Hearing that was a surprise, but it changed nothing. If I couldn't fight them, she couldn't either. They'd just fire her and replace her as easily as they were ousting me.

"Tell me about it," I grunted, and I laid my head back against the wall again.

"I mean, if you fight this, you could win. There is actually a paper trail indicating that someone else didn't update the patient's files the way they were supposed to." Her voice grew so quiet I almost had to strain to hear her. I turned my head and narrowed my eyes on her.

"What do you mean?" If the board was withholding information in this lawsuit that would clear me, I was going to be livid.

"I mean, they pay me to watch out for them, but I think it's disgusting. You don't deserve what they're doing, and I think you should seek legal representation before they tell the patient that their investigation has fingered you." Her tone was so hushed now, I knew she was scared of losing her job over this. "And I think you should do it soon."

So I had the one decent human being to ever take a position as HR advocating for me for a change, but it still felt impossible. I had the money to fight this but Premier Health was a huge organization. Twin Peaks was only one of their hundreds of hospitals. They could bury this easily, pay off the patient and make it go away, but they wanted someone to take the fall instead. They weren't going down without a fight.

"Thank you for telling me that..." I closed my eyes again and sighed. there was no point in hanging her up in this. "You should go before one of the board members sees you talking to me and figures out you're on my side." I knew two of the board members personally— self-righteous jerks who'd definitely go for the jugular with her if they saw her cluing me in.

"Alright... Just... I'm sorry," she said in a rushed voice as she stood and tucked her laptop under her arm and walked away. I watched her scurry like a church mouse and sighed.

The entire thing pissed me off and I felt powerless to fight the giant. But if she thought hiring a lawyer would help, it was probably a good idea. I knew I hadn't done anything wrong, but this slight tremor in my hand would tell a different story. The board would find out and that would be it. They would fire me without hesitation and leave me to defend myself. As it was, right now, the hospital's legal team was handling things, but even they weren't fighting for me. They just wanted the suit to go away.

I made it to my office and locked myself in. The lights were off, and I left them off as I sank into my desk chair and raked both hands through my hair and then down over my face. Each day that passed brought more bad news from that front and more challenges as I faced surgeries with the fear that my tremors would be noticed and pointed out, or worse, that I would make a real mistake because of them and hurt someone.

I found a clinic in Kansas City, Missouri, that would do the testing and diagnostics for me discreetly. It was outside of the Premier Health network, and my records could be sealed there and not shared with any of my insurance providers or my bosses here, but it would mean taking a short trip from work. That would only raise questions, so I'd been hesitating.

I was just torn. I knew I needed to do the right thing, but with this threat of a lawsuit looming, it felt like the right thing was the hard thing and it would destroy my career. All of the back and forth felt like it was consuming my time and energy, and I felt frustrated and distracted.

Until I thought of Rose.

Each time she crossed my mind, I paused to take a deep breath and smile. Like a ray of sunshine in the middle of a storm, she brought me peace and stability in this chaos. Thinking of the way we connected and how she made me feel capable and in control again made me desire to speak with her and be around her, and it was a small comfort I needed.

I rose and walked out of my office deciding to go in search of her. But my brooding mood went with me. I walked through the oncology ward where she typically worked, but she wasn't around. So I breezed through pediatrics, where I'd also seen her. My mood was growing worse by the minute, but I held out hope that if and when I did see her, she'd accept my invitation to join me for dinner again.

After twenty minutes of searching to no avail, I walked out to the employee break area outside and sat down, and moments later, Rose approached me. She carried a smoothie in her hand and her ponytail swung behind her.

"Hey, Cole," she said, and even though I wanted to see her and talk to her, her chipper tone grated on my bruised ego.

"Yeah," I grunted, not wanting to be grumpy with her but not knowing how to change my mood.

"Is everything okay?" she asked softly, and she sat down next to me. She smelled good and that softened my edge, but thoughts of the board meeting still burned my conscience.

"Uh, not really, but I'm just not in the mood to talk about it." Out of the corner of my eye, I saw her wince and her head dropped.

"Sorry, I just thought... Uh, it's okay." Rose stood and faced me. "I'll catch you later?"

She looked hurt, and I felt guilty.

"I'm sorry, this isn't your fault. It's something I'm dealing with right now." I stood next to her, and she smiled again.

"It's okay. I understand..."

"I was just thinking how well dinner went last week and maybe you'd want to do it again?" The comfort of her presence was what I was craving. I missed having someone to come home to and talk about my day. While I didn't think I could or should open up about what was going on, at least the distraction of her sweet smile and conversation would help me get my mind off things for a while.

"I'd love that... Friday night?" she asked, and she tilted her head to the side.

"Sounds good. I really am sorry for being grumpy," I told her again, and she patted my arm.

"Go have a run. That's what I do when I'm down." Rose turned and walked away, and I wished it were Friday already. Hiding from my reality wasn't a good coping strategy, but at least it worked for a while.

Now I had to find a lawyer and figure out how to fight this giant, and I had to make a plan to get to Kansas city and get something to help with these tremors before I really did lose everything. Getting fired and being unemployable wasn't a good look, and no woman would want to date me then. Not even a powerhouse like Rose.

1 2

ROSE

I carried the weight of that interaction with Cole on my shoulders as I walked back into the hospital after my break. I had never seen him that irritable before, but I knew everyone had bad days now and then. It felt a little off putting, but I didn't know everything about him, only what little he had shared and what Kiki had told me. Now I wondered what sort of things could be happening in his life to make him so grumpy and if there was a way I could help.

I headed to the nurse's station to check back in and overheard them chatting about something. It piqued my interest and I felt bad, but I listened in a little.

"Well you know what's coming next. If that lawsuit goes through, they'll cut nursing. No way they go to cutting doctors. They'll just expect us to work more hours for the same pay and have fewer hands to do the work." One of the nurses, a frumpy woman named Pam, looked upset. I didn't know what lawsuit they were talking about, but hearing that bit about firing nurses caught my attention. I couldn't just ignore that.

"What did you say?" I asked, turning to pick up a stack of charts I had to file. The nurse looked up at me, and so did the younger one. This was when I hated my own policy of not making friends with coworkers. I intentionally did not learn their names so I could feel less attached. Now I wish I knew them.

The younger nurse, *Ginny*, her nametag read, said, "Oh, some doctor screwed up and there's a malpractice suit out there. If Premier Health gets sued, there'll be hell to pay. I've never dealt with this, but Pam has and—

"And it's not pretty," Pam said, cutting Ginny off. She scowled. "They have to come up with money somewhere, and you know they won't stop their research or expensive testing that's unnecessary. They'll just cut laborers. Doctors are too important so they cut nursing and techs, and that leaves us in a pinch." I wasn't fond of her negative attitude, but I was listening to her words.

"Wow, yeah. That doesn't sound good." I wanted to ask if they knew what happened, but I felt like that was bordering on gossip. If hospital administration wanted us to know, they would announce it. I grimaced and backed a step away. "Thanks... Uh, if that happens, who gets fired first?"

"Well, it's not like firing," Ginny said. "They call it reduction in force, and you're just laid off. You'd be free to work somewhere else, but you can't draw unemployment for a year." She sighed hard and shook her head.

"That's awful," I mumbled, and Pam picked up where Ginny left off.

"Yeah, and the first ones hired are the first to go. So, lucky me, since I've been here twenty-two years, I get to do all your work." Pam was projecting her anger about the hospital's policy onto me because I was the new girl, and I didn't like that at all. But some people were just rude like that.

I turned and walked away with my new knowledge, but it made my footsteps heavy.

After Cole's grumpiness, I felt even more weighted now. I knew I couldn't control the future and that there was no point in worrying about things, but I needed this job. Hearing that things higher up the food chain were happening to put my job at risk made me feel uneasy as I filed the charts away and turned toward my first patient.

Her name was Bethany, a sixteen-year-old girl who came in with a broken femur after a soccer match. She was bright and full of life, and I loved stopping by to see her. I popped into her room and she was all smiles, sitting up in bed.

"Hey, Bethany, how are you feeling today?" She had only a few more days left and she could go home. Her days were spent lonely while her parents worked, but they came by for dinner in the evenings. We just had to get her fitted for a walker and able to move around a bit by herself and she'd be gone.

"Oh, hey, Rose. I'm doing so much better. When Ginny came in to help me use the toilet, I just used the wheelchair, but I'm really looking forward to being up on my feet again." I was amazed by how this girl in her teens took this all in stride. She lost her ability to play her favorite sport during her junior year and she was still positive. It was a real reminder to me that no matter what happened, I'd be fine.

"That's so good. I heard ortho is coming in this afternoon to bring you a few different types of walkers and crutches. You follow your rehab schedule and you'll be training for soccer again by fall. It's sad you'll miss the spring league, though." I turned to check her wristband and then checked that against the computer to make sure she was getting her proper pain meds. Everything was in order, but she was so positive all the time, I just liked being in her room.

"Oh, that's nothing. I'll be fine for senior year. The scouts will be out to watch, I'm sure." She smiled broadly and said, "Hey, do you mind getting me some more of that Jell-O? I'm feeling hungry today."

"Absolutely," I told her, grinning. "I'll be right back." I stepped into the hallway and walked around the corner to the nurses' station. We kept cups of Jell-O in the fridge for patients, so I walked in to get one and while I was in there, I heard someone whistle under their breath. I poked my head out, cup of Jell-O in hand, and saw Cole walking past.

"Lordy, lordy... Dr. Silver Fox is on it today. Look at that brooding expression. He's like a real fox stalking prey." Pam waggled her eyebrows, and Ginny chuckled.

"He could come stalk me any day." Ginny snickered and fanned herself. Jealousy pinched my chest, and I scowled a little. They had every right to look at him or talk the way they wanted, but it sort of left me feeling miffed, considering I was seeing him but we couldn't—or shouldn't—say anything.

I stood just inside the kitchenette doorway and listened to them talking, hating that I was eavesdropping but unable to walk away. I had no claim staked on Dr. Hastings. He was a free man, but for some reason, I felt possessive, like I was upset they were even looking at him.

"I heard Hicks and Davidson both got fired for shacking up, Gin. I wouldn't be getting any fancy imaginations about the sexy silver fox." Pam's words of caution aimed at Ginny hit me square in the chest. I'd never met the two employees she was speaking of, but it didn't get past me that they were "shacking up" and got fired for it.

Cole said we'd be fine because we worked in different departments, but I'd had my hesitation. Policy was policy, and if the hospital HR team wanted to get nitpicky, they could.

"I was just fantasizing, Pam." Ginny's tone was playfully chastising, but I heard the tinge of disappointment in her tone.

I wondered how many nurses had fantasized about Cole and how many had told him. How many times a day did he have to fend off would-be paramours to keep himself out of trouble? I didn't like that feeling at all.

"I'm just reminding you to walk the line. With the hospital under scrutiny, now isn't the time to go all *Girls Gone Wild*. If you know what I mean."

I scowled and swallowed the lump in my throat as I left the kitchenette and ignored the looks Ginny and Pam gave me. I felt like I was on an emotional yo-yo from one moment to the next, and I wanted to stop and get off.

I walked with the Jell-O back to Bethany's room, but I was the one brooding now. Pam had a really good point. Not only was I one of the last nurses to be hired recently, but I was also walking on thin ice. If the hospital did start laying off nurses, I couldn't really afford to be the first out the door. Bethany was encouraging with her spirit, but she was sixteen. She didn't have bills to pay. I was risking my career by sneaking around with a coworker.

I started thinking, maybe this wasn't a good idea. Maybe if the hospital was on the verge of major cuts, I shouldn't be putting a large red target on my back. But the idea of letting Cole down when he was going through something, and especially if what Kiki said was true about his not opening up to anyone or dating… I felt stuck.

And that wasn't a good feeling to have.

13

COLE

I stood over my stove adding salt and spices to the food in the skillet. Rose leaned against my kitchen counter looking a bit apprehensive. I'd opted for a meal at home instead of a restaurant this time to avoid anyone from work spotting us. While I wasn't exactly nervous about that particular thing, I knew she was a bit hesitant. And with the heat on my position at work, it was a good idea to take a play from her book and be cautious, at the very least.

"So you seem in a better mood tonight," she said, and I sighed, pushing some of my negative thoughts away. I'd managed to destress a little since the other day when I asked her to have dinner with me.

"Yeah, it's been a tough week, but it's over and you're here now." I smiled at her warmly and turned back to my work. The stir fry smelled delicious and I couldn't wait to dig in, but I was enjoying the discussion with Rose while I cooked.

"I'm sure it's personal, but I'm here if you want to talk." She shrugged one shoulder, and I glanced up at her. It was kind of her to offer, but I still wondered what she'd say if she knew I was the doctor who messed up and put the entire nursing staff at risk. There were rumors that the administration would start making cuts if the lawsuit went through.

"I'm really okay, but thank you for offering." My hand shook a little as I stirred the dish with the wooden spoon, and some grease splashed up and landed on my arm. I dropped the spoon on the stove and yelped in pain, rushing right to the sink.

Cold water soothed the small burn immediately but did nothing to cool the shame burning in my chest. I plunged my hand under the icy flow and bit down on the inside of my cheek to stifle the grumble of anger I felt rising up.

"Oh, my God, are you okay?" she asked, and she was there, holding my hand, nursing me the way she was trained to do. "Wow, this is second degree. Do you have a first-aid kit?" she asked, and her eyes met mine. I felt so foolish.

"Uh, no," I admitted, and she frowned.

"What happened?" Her eyes went back to looking at the wound, still under the flow of water.

"I'm a klutz," I said, forcing a chuckle. It masked the way I really felt, like a total waste of humanity. I was a surgeon. I was supposed to have steady hands, and here I was, bumbling up my own dinner. How was I supposed to keep this a secret from the nursing staff I worked with if it was getting worse like this?

Rose laughed and pulled my hand out from under the water, pressing a hand towel to it. She reached for the dish soap and rubbed a small amount on it, then rinsed it for me. When she dried it the second time she said, "Bandages, at least?" Her eyebrows rose, and I pointed a thumb over my shoulder.

"Bathroom medicine cabinet. Second door on the left."

She dashed off to get a bandage, and I turned the heat under the pan down on low. I hadn't felt this low in my entire life, and that was saying something following Kate... The idea that I could lose my career over something I had no control over was gutting. I didn't know how to keep myself emotionally stable. I felt torn between crawling into bed and never getting out again and going on a rampage, smashing things because it would at least burn off some of this energy.

I stirred the food in silence, stewing over how I was going to get the treatment I needed. With everything going on at work, I wasn't sure if I should take the time off right now. I would have to have a reason to leave town during work time, but my weekends were busy now too. Rose and I were bonding, and that was when I spent my time with her.

When she came back and pried me away from the stove to put the bandage on my hand, she looked sad. I felt sorry for worrying her like this, but my gut told me that wasn't the only reason she was feeling down.

"What is it?" I asked her, and I took a chance and pulled her onto my lap. She lazily draped her arms around my shoulders while I reached to shut off the stove. We sat at the small dining table in my eat-in kitchen, and I felt like bad news was coming.

"Cole, I'm just worried. I know you said that we are in different departments so people at work will never suspect us, but I'm worried that our seeing each other might be detrimental to my job. I heard another couple was busted 'shacking up,' as Pam told me. They both got fired." She bit her lip and grimaced, and I sighed. I held her tightly, unwilling to let her go.

She was the first woman since Kate whom I'd even looked at twice, the only one who caught my attention. Yes, she was gorgeous, but it wasn't that. Rose was charming and funny, and when she smiled, it lit up the whole room. Just having her near me made me feel better.

"I feel like the best way to keep things a secret is to do them in secret..." My mind started whirring with ideas. I wanted to be around her, and she wanted to be around me—I thought. Despite her fear, at least. What if she went with me to Kansas City? I could do my treatment and send her for a spa day. No one would know where we went. It was our weekend to plan, and we'd have time together without missing a beat. Plus, it would be completely private, keeping her job safe.

She narrowed her eyes on me. "What do you mean?"

My hand palmed her ass cheek and I grinned at her. "Rose, you have no idea the change you've brought into my life. I want to see where this goes, even if it means we have to take a risk. I can find a new job. They're a dime a dozen for a man like me." That line made bile rise up in the back of my throat because right now, that part wasn't exactly true. I was walking a line here. "But a good woman is so hard to find, one in a million."

She teared up a little. "You think I'm one in a million?" Her voice was so soft, filled with emotion, and I had to pull her down for a kiss.

"Honestly, I don't think that—I know that. Don't make me have to beg you..." I kissed her again, and she let her hand run up the back of my head into my hair. It was a good feeling having someone in my arms again, and I was thrilled the woman on my lap was as amazing as she was. Everything else I said was true. I really did want to see where this went. Even if we had to do it privately.

"What do you want to do, then?" she asked when she pulled away. I squeezed her ass again and thought about it for a second.

"Well, we can't exactly screw in the broom closet. We'd get caught..." Rose chuckled at me again, and I continued. "So how about we go away for a weekend? I know this great little spa in Kansas City. I think you'll love it."

Rose's face lit up and she grinned at me. "You want to take me away for a weekend?"

"Yeah, why not? I've been looking for an excuse to get away for a weekend. I think we'll have a great time." The idea was settling on me now, feeling like the right choice. I could get my checkup and treatment underway, which would help me at least get the stress of the tremors off my shoulders, and she and I could bond more, hopefully putting all her fears to bed.

Deep down, I knew it was a little selfish, but my heart just craved a little comfort in the middle of this stress. I wanted her to be the one to comfort me. And I knew there was a spark between us that we shouldn't ignore.

"You want to sneak around with me like we're teenagers avoiding getting into trouble?" The question would have bothered me, except I could tell she was enjoying this by the grin on her face.

"Only because the sex is so incredible," I said, grinning.

"Oh, you like my sex, do you?" The little vixen was pushing every button I had. This sexy hard-to-get act had my dick hard and throbbing, and I wanted to stroke it and watch her touch herself.

"Yeah, enough to bend you over this table right now." I squeezed her ass hard again, and she leaned down to kiss me again. Dinner was getting cold, but I could always reheat it. This idea of going away for a weekend together and my finally getting to see that specialist at the clinic made me happy.

"Oh, go ahead and make me..." The way she challenged me only got me going more. I stood, taking her with me, and started undressing her instantly. Her skin seemed to ignite under my fingertips, and it made my dick throb.

Rose gasped but she didn't fight me. In fact, she got as hot and bothered by it as I was, kissing me while tearing into my clothing.

70

"You know," I said, my voice deep and husky as I slid her panties down her thighs, "I want to fuck you on this table."

"Yeah?" she said, her voice breathless as I teased her aching clit with my fingers.

"Yeah... And on the counter, and on the couch..." I kissed her again hard, and she managed to shove my pants down. They slid down my legs and I stepped out of them as she pulled my shirt over my head. My cock stood erect, begging for her pussy, and I wondered how long I'd last.

"This is more than just sex, though... Right?" I hated that she felt insecure about that, so I paused and cupped her cheek. My eyes searched her expression. I never wanted her to feel like a toy.

"I'll stop right now if you want. Rose, I want more than just sex with you. Meeting you was the best thing to happen to me in years." Her eyes explored mine, and she guided my hand back to her clit. She was soaked. I was so horny.

"Then show me how grateful you are." Her lips crushed against mine, and I growled low in my chest as I kissed her and bit her lip.

"Oh, I'll show you grateful," I whispered against her ear before picking her up and laying her down on the table. I spread her legs apart and lowered to my knees, diving into her folds. She tasted sweet like cream and salty like caramel. I groaned against her, my tongue lapping up every drop of her arousal.

Rose moaned, her nails digging into my shoulders as I continued to tease her mercilessly. I loved how wet she got for me and how she didn't try to hide it.

"Oh, God, I can't..." she whined.

"Yeah, come for me, Rose. Let me taste your sweetness," I said against her core before sucking hard on her clit. Her back arched off the table and she gasped in pleasure. I slid a few fingers into her and teased her a little before I started thrusting. I loved the way she squirmed and moaned under me, all incoherent words and moans.

Rose's orgasm crashed through her like a tidal wave, and she grunted my name as her juices flooded my mouth. I didn't stop, even when she was spent, until she pushed me away, gasping for air.

"Oh, God," she panted, "I love the way you eat me."

"Mm-hmm," I said, licking my fingers clean. "You taste delicious." I stood up and positioned myself at her entrance. "Now, are you ready for the main course?"

"Oh, fuck yes," Rose purred.

I slid into her wet heat slowly and steadily, savoring every single inch of her tightness. "You feel so good," I groaned, burying myself deep inside her.

"I love the way you fill me," she moaned. Her hands clung to my sides, nails digging into my flesh. I slid in and out of her with practiced ease. The rhythm I set was comfortable, and Rose rubbed her clit while I fucked her.

I got lost in her, kissing, groping, kneading her breasts. She panted and whimpered my name, driving herself toward climax again, and when she came undone around my dick, it was all I could do to hold off. No condom meant a risk, and we'd already done that once. The very instant I felt my balls drawing up, I pulled out, shooting wads of stringy white cum onto her stomach. She gripped my dick and stroked me, milking the last few drops out, before sitting up and grinning at me.

"I worked up an appetite, Doctor. Maybe you should feed me before my examination. I'm going to need a full checkup." She winked at me and grabbed the hand towel she'd used to clean my burn and wiped my cum off her stomach. Then she slid off the table, kissed me and licked her juices off my lips, and then picked up her clothing and walked toward the bathroom.

I didn't know what I did to deserve such a wild little minx, but I loved it. The sex, the comfort, the distraction—she was everything I could ever ask for and more. And going into the fight of my life, I needed that. I just had to make sure I helped her feel safe and told her a million times how I couldn't do this without her.

Because I knew I couldn't. It was going to challenge me to my core.

ROSE

A s I pulled the load of laundry out of the dryer into a basket, I could still hear Alana telling her boyfriend, Rick, how big of a mistake I was making. I scowled, though I hid it from her because I didn't want her to get annoyed with me. She acted like she was my mother, but I knew it came from a place of fear.

Alana was convinced that I was going to blow it and lose my job. It had taken so long to secure this job in the city that paid well enough for me to help with rent. If I lost it, there was a good chance I'd have to go searching for something new, which would be an impossible task. I could get a million jobs, but none of them paid well enough to afford anything. Which meant I'd have to have two jobs, and getting two jobs that would work together to balance my hours would be difficult too.

I regretted telling her. I'd let it slip on Wednesday evening while we were watching TV. I sat beside her with a glass of wine while she and Rick were necking. When Cole messaged me something naughty about this weekend, I grinned at my phone and Alana asked what it was about. They all but pried it out of me. It was like they had this magical ability to know what had happened and dog me about it.

I picked up the basket and carried it toward my bedroom. I had to pass by the living room and the couch where Alana sat on Rick's lap again, cuddling and talking. I wished Cole and I could do that, but I doubted very much that a wealthy, successful doctor would want to come to this tiny little apartment. Besides, he was old enough for a mortgage and I was struggling to get my life started. And the last thing I needed was Alana laying in on him about propriety and our age difference.

"I still can't believe you're going..." Her tone wasn't lecturing or nagging. It sounded more like disillusionment. She really thought Cole was just using me to get off, that he was just a player wanting nothing but sex from me. I'd never shake that idea from her mind. "Rose, you need to protect yourself. You don't know what sort of person he is."

"It's okay, Alana," Rick said, smirking at me. "Just let her screw up and lose her job. Then there will be room for me to move in. I can help pay rent."

I gritted my teeth instead of biting back, but he really pushed my buttons with that comment. I was actually nervous that it could be a reality, and the reminder made me want to lash out at him. I knew the anger wasn't my actual emotion. I was just afraid deep down and unsure about my choices.

"I'm not going to lose my job." I turned to face them, tamping my frustration down. "Cole is a sweet man, and I think we could really have something." The fact that Alana and I had only known each other a short time hadn't escaped my mind.

We gelled right away when I moved in, but maybe I was a fool to truly trust her. I knew she had her own fears and worries, but I felt like she wasn't thinking of how I'd feel in this situation. But she knew me only as well as I knew her, so I had to cut her some slack.

"I'm just saying, Rose. I know you come from a small town and stuff, so I just want you to be aware that not all men are wholesome or have your best interests at heart." The look of genuine concern made me nod politely, but it didn't stop the frustration.

I turned and carried my basket of laundry into my room and set it on the foot of my bed. As far as I was concerned, Alana was being too critical. She didn't know Cole. She'd never even met him. All she knew about him was that he was an older man with great looks and money.

I'd seen his heart. I'd seen the way his emotions leaked out when he spoke of his late wife. I'd seen how the stresses of life were weighing his shoulders, and I'd seen how his face lit up when he asked me to go away for the weekend with him. Those were all true green flags to me. A man interested in manipulating me for just sex wouldn't be so vulnerable like that.

The point Rick made, however, did still nag at my conscience. I knew Cole said we could just keep our relationship private, but I worried about people at work finding out. The thought of that couple who got fired for having a secret relationship just kept niggling at my nerves, making me so anxious. I knew there was an almost zero-percent chance that anyone we knew would see us this weekend, but it wasn't about this weekend.

My fear was more about what I'd do when we got back here to Denver and had to hide our relationship. How would we cope with or manage the work-life balance without seeming overly friendly or connected? And was that really the type of relationship I wanted to have? Did I really want to have to hide the love of my life from my coworkers— assuming Cole and I ended up really falling for each other?

I packed while my mind toiled away, and I still had massive doubts about all of this when Cole called me. I saw the number and sighed before answering.

"Hey," I said, letting my true anticipation sound through my tone.

"Are you all packed and ready?" he asked, and I glanced at my alarm clock on my nightstand. It was almost six, the time he said he'd come get me. We had to get through security to board our plane by eight. I wasn't quite there, but I knew he had a fifteen-minute drive to my place, so I had time to shove a few more things in the bag and tie my hair back.

"Just doing the last of my packing. You can come anytime." My racing thoughts wanted to come out in a rush of rambling questions and insecurities, but I tamped them down.

"Great. Give me a few more minutes and I'll be headed your way. I'm really looking forward to the time alone with you. I can't wait." Cole sounded so happy, and after what Kiki told me about his not opening up or letting anyone in after his wife's death years ago, I knew that was a good thing. It brought my heart true joy.

"I can't wait either." I said my goodbyes and hung up, and my entire perspective about this weekend shifted. I liked Cole for way more than just the way he made me feel sexually. We could sit and talk about anything and get along. He had his life together and was responsible and mature, and most of all, we had a lot in common. This could really end up being something, and I didn't want to dismiss the bond I was forming because I was afraid.

I shoved a few more things into my suitcase and zipped it up. Then I went into my bathroom and tied my hair up into a messy bun and found a few more things I'd missed. This weekend was going to be amazing, even if I had to fight my own doubts.

When you found someone you genuinely connected with, you weren't supposed to run away because circumstances weren't right. Relationships were about commitment, faithfulness, hard work, and a promise to overcome all the obstacles in your path in order to make things work and be with the person. If we started this relationship with my shying away, it didn't bode well for the longevity of things.

I was going to make this weekend fantastic, and when we came back, I'd decide whether it was worth the risk. I'd never know if I didn't try.

15

COLE

The restaurant gleamed with the kind of quiet elegance that whispered exclusivity. Low amber lighting spilled across polished tables and deep leather booths, and the faint clink of crystal glasses underscored the hum of murmured conversations. The scent of something decadent—truffle oil, maybe—hung in the air. It was the kind of place where even breathing felt like a luxury.

Rose walked a step ahead of me, her red dress shifting like poured wine under the dim glow. My pulse stuttered as she turned, her lips curving into a smile that made the ambient warmth of the room feel irrelevant.

"Cole, are you always this quiet before a meal, or is this restaurant just intimidating you?" she teased, her eyes alight with mischief.

I chuckled, pulling out her chair. "I'm just savoring the moment. And by that, I mean you. The restaurant's just a backdrop."

She rolled her eyes but didn't hide her blush. "Smooth."

As I sat opposite her, the waiter glided over with menus, and I caught my reflection in the mirrored wall behind him. I looked like a man trying not to fall too hard, too fast. The problem was, I was already gone. I knew it before we even planned this weekend. Rose was dangerous for me because it meant opening my heart to the possibility that I could hurt again. But to love meant to hurt, and yet I wanted to take the risk anyway.

"This is really pricey," she said, staring down at the large, unpronounceable words.

I chuckled and admired how honest she was. Her youthful openness was invigorating, reminding me of what young love felt like. I wasn't as young as I used to be, but she helped me feel more youthful.

"Just say spaghetti," I told her, winking. Rose snickered and used the menu to hide her face, giving me a chance to check my phone.

It buzzed when we were on the elevator down to dinner. I had ignored it then, eliminating the risk of her seeing what it said on the chance it was a reminder from the clinic. When I pulled my phone from my pocket, I had never been more glad that I had made that choice. The text was a reminder about the appointment and I had to take a breath to keep myself calm.

I had been nervous all week about this appointment. I knew it could go one of two ways. Either the doctor was going to say we could use medications to help me reverse symptoms and keep control of my life a while longer, or he was going to say it was the end of the line for my career. No one knew why tremors like this happened, though they did have some treatments. I just hoped the tremors were really what I thought and not something worse like MS or Parkinson's.

"Who's that?" Rose asked, and I hadn't even realized she was watching me stare at my phone.

"Oh, just a reminder for your spa day tomorrow." I smiled at her and put my phone away.

Rose beamed. She pushed a lock of her warm brown hair off her shoulders and grinned at me. "I am actually really excited about that. I've never spoiled myself with a spa day."

"Well, good," I said, happy to have something to discuss that kept my mind off the appointment. Our waiter came and brought us bread and took our orders. We filled our glasses with wine and chatted about the spa treatments available. Rose was worried it would take too long and I'd be bored, and I assured her that I had something to do.

The waiter had just left, and a flicker of candlelight danced on the surface of my wine as I set the glass down. Across from me, Rose leaned back in her chair, tracing the stem of her glass with her fingertips. The bottle sat between us, already missing enough that I knew she was savoring the edge of tipsiness.

"I'll say it," she began, a sly smile playing on her lips. "This place? Way too fancy for me."

I raised an eyebrow. "Too fancy? You're sitting there looking like you own it."

She gave me a skeptical look, lifting her glass. "Please. They probably saw me walk in and thought, 'Well, there goes the neighborhood.'"

I smirked, resting my chin on one hand. "If anything, they're upgrading the neighborhood. They're probably back there renaming the house special after you."

"Oh, yeah? The Rose Special?" She swirled her wine dramatically. "What would that even be? A glass of this stuff and a plate of fries?"

The waiter returned with our plates, setting down her roasted salmon and my steak with the kind of precision that made me wonder if they took a geometry class before waiter training. The smells of rosemary and butter filled the air.

"Fries might clash a bit," I said as I picked up my fork. "But if anyone could make it work, it's you."

Rose tilted her head, cutting into her salmon with deliberate care. "You're laying it on thick tonight, Cole. Is this a regular thing for you, or do I just bring it out of you?"

I shrugged, cutting into my steak. "You? Definitely you. And maybe the wine."

"Mm," she said, taking a sip. "Good answer. I'm feeling generous, so I'll allow it."

The conversation flowed as easily as the wine. Rose, I realized, was the kind of person who could make a debate about buttered bread feel like an art form. By the time she poured herself a second glass, she'd just finished recounting a disastrous childhood spelling bee story that had me grinning so hard my face hurt.

"Okay," I said, setting my fork down, "but you left out the key part. Did you recover and win, or was that the end of Rose the Spelling Bee Queen?"

She groaned, laughing. "I got eliminated! I misspelled 'rhythm'. I still hate that word."

"It's a cruel one. Sneaky, silent letters," I said sympathetically.

She held up her glass, her eyes sparkling. "Thank you. Finally, someone who understands my pain."

I clinked my glass against hers. "To overcoming childhood trauma."

Rose giggled, sipping again. She was starting to loosen up, leaning forward with her elbow on the table now, her chin resting in her hand. "You know," she said, her voice dipping into something softer, "you're really cute when you smile like that."

I blinked, taken off guard, and she laughed, clearly enjoying my reaction. "Oh, don't get shy on me now," she teased.

"I'm not shy," I said, recovering quickly. "Just trying to figure out whether this is the wine talking or you."

She leaned in just slightly, her gaze locking onto mine. "It's me. But the wine's definitely cheering me on."

She was adorable when she snickered and filled her glass a third time, and I felt like I was definitely going to get lucky tonight. We continued to talk and flirt until her plate was empty, and so was the bottle. When she announced that she was feeling like having privacy with me, I flagged our waiter down and paid our tab, then escorted her to the elevator.

The moment the elevator doors closed, she was all over me, her red dress swirling around her thighs as she wrapped her legs around my waist. I didn't know when I'd last been so turned on by a woman, but Rose was fire in a dress. I lifted her up and pressed her against the wall, kissing her like my life depended on it.

Her lips were soft and sweet, but beneath them I could taste the heady desire that matched my own. Her hands slid under my suit jacket and then down to my shirt buttons, unfastening them one by one as we continued to make out in the confined space. By the time we reached our floor, I was breathless and ready to have her right there against the wall.

But self-control won out—barely—and I managed to carry her out of the elevator and down the hallway to the room. I fumbled with the keycard, finally sliding it into the reader and opening the door. Inside, I kicked it shut behind us and didn't bother to turn on the lights.

In the dim glow of the cityscape outside my window, I kissed her, head arched back, mouth agape. I carried her to the bed and laid her down, but her arms weren't reaching for me as greedily anymore. They still clung to me, and her lips still moved against mine as I lay on top of her and let my weight rest on her body, but I could tell she was too far gone. She had drunk too much too quickly, and I had to do the right thing no matter how badly I wanted her.

I pulled away and she whimpered, but I knew it was the right choice. I rolled her to her side and unzipped the dress, and when I began to shimmy it down over her curves, she pulled my face down to her chest. I kissed her lightly, suckling a nipple and driving myself wild with desire, but I felt her slipping off to sleep.

I got the dress off her, let her shoes drop to the floor. Then I undid the clasp of her necklace, fumbling with it several minutes before finally getting it off her, and managed to get her under the covers. When she was situated and snoring softly, I took off my clothes, down to my boxers, set my alarm, turned the heater down to a comfortable sleeping temperature, and returned to bed to hold her.

My mind immediately went to my appointment tomorrow. I knew it would take a few hours for her at the spa, and I had a one-hour session with the specialist. My entire career was riding on it and I was genuinely concerned. Some would say I was scared. Men weren't supposed to get scared at all. they were supposed to be strong and have their shit together, but the idea of losing my ability to perform surgery wasn't anywhere in my future plans.

I just hoped I could hold my shit together long enough to get Rose off to her spa day. I lay there thinking about what an idiot I was for dragging her into my mess and how I'd never forgive myself if I made her life worse by doing it.

16

ROSE

The spa was everything I imagined luxury would feel like— and more. From the moment I stepped through the frosted glass doors, a wave of lavender and eucalyptus greeted me, as if the air itself had been designed to exhale my stress. The receptionist, a woman with a smooth voice and a name tag that read *Celeste*, handed me a plush white robe and slippers as she explained my deluxe package with the kind of care usually reserved for unwrapping delicate presents.

"This includes a full-body massage, a facial, and access to the relaxation lounge. You're going to love it," she said, her smile so serene it made me wonder if working here came with mandatory Zen training.

I nodded, trying to play it cool even as excitement bubbled beneath my skin. "Sounds perfect."

She led me down a hallway where soft instrumental music drifted, mingling with the faint trickle of a fountain I couldn't see but somehow felt. The walls were painted in calming shades of cream and taupe, with flickering candles tucked into alcoves every few feet.

When I was shown to a room, my masseuse—a woman named Lena with hands that could probably sculpt clouds—welcomed me warmly.

"First time?" she asked kindly, her eyes crinkling with a knowing smile.

"Is it that obvious?" I laughed, shrugging into the robe.

"Don't worry," Lena said, her voice as soothing as the ambiance. "We'll make sure it's unforgettable."

As I settled onto the heated massage table, a wave of nausea hit me out of nowhere. It wasn't overwhelming, but enough to make my stomach twist uncomfortably. I closed my eyes, breathing in the lavender-scented air and blaming last night's wine. I knew I'd gone overboard, so maybe I wasn't as invincible as I used to be.

Lena's hands began working on my shoulders, and though the pressure was perfect, the queasiness lingered. I frowned, recalling how I'd been unusually tired lately, too—like I could nap at any moment. Probably just stress or something. Right? Still, it was hard to ignore.

I pushed away the thoughts and closed my eyes. Last night, Cole had been such a gentleman. I was so horny, wanted him so badly. I'd have let him fuck me right there in the elevator, but he insisted on carrying me to the room, and by the time we got there, I was just too drunk. I felt him undress me and tuck me in, but I never felt him climb into bed. I was so wasted, which only confirmed my initial thought. The nausea was a hangover and nothing more.

My phone, in my purse across the room where I left it when I put on the robe, began to ring. It was a ringtone I assigned to my mother, and she rarely called so I felt like I should take it. I lifted my head and looked that direction and Lena said, "Want me to get that for you?"

"Would you please?" I asked her, not really sure if this was a thing or not. I felt bad because I didn't know if they had a no phones policy, but it was my mom.

Lena reached into my purse and pulled out my phone, and as soon as she handed it to me, I answered.

"Hi, Mom," I said, holding the phone to my ear.

"Rose! Are you busy? I hope I'm not interrupting anything," she said, the way moms always do when they know they absolutely are.

"Not really," I replied, keeping my voice light. "I'm at this amazing spa Cole brought me to. Seriously, you wouldn't believe this place—it smells like a lavender field and a rainforest had a baby."

There was a brief pause, just long enough for me to brace myself. "Cole?" she asked, the curiosity sharp in her tone. "I don't think you've mentioned him before."

I hesitated, realizing she was right. This was the first time I'd said his name to her. "Oh. Yeah, I guess I haven't. He's... kind of new, but not really. We've been seeing each other for a few months."

"A few months, and you're just now telling me?" she asked, half teasing, half concerned. "What's he like? And how old is 'new, but not really'?"

I bit my lip, trying to figure out how to play this. "Okay, first, he's amazing. Like, genuinely incredible. He's kind and thoughtful and..." I trailed off, smiling despite myself. "He's just got this way about him, you know? Like he knows exactly how to make me feel comfortable and safe."

"Mmhmm," she murmured, clearly not sold yet. "And?"

"And..." I drew the word out, hesitant. "He's a little older than me."

"How much older?"

"Fifteen years," I said quickly, wincing as I braced for her reaction.

"Fifteen?" she repeated, her voice rising slightly. "Rose, that's... that's a big gap."

"I know it sounds like a lot," I said, rushing to fill the silence, "but it's not weird. It doesn't feel weird. He's—he's grounded in this way that I've never had in a relationship before. And I need that, Mom. After all the guys who were, like, obsessed with video games or afraid of commitment, Cole's refreshing."

She exhaled, the sound heavy with caution. "Okay. So he's older. What does he do?"

"He's a surgeon," I said, knowing it would impress her but also anticipating the next wave of concern. Lena glanced at me with a professional poker face, probably used to people rambling on their phones mid-massage. I gave her an apologetic smile and let my head sink back down.

"A surgeon?" Her tone was skeptical, but I caught the faintest note of admiration. "Well, that's… respectable. But don't you think there's a power imbalance there, Rose? Older man, successful career, bringing you to fancy spas… He could be trying to, I don't know, control things."

"Mom, stop," I said, laughing despite myself. "It's not like that. Cole's not manipulative. He's supportive, and he listens to me. Honestly, he's probably more patient with me than anyone else ever has been." I sighed, closing my eyes as Lena worked on a knot in my neck.

"That's nice," she said carefully, but I could hear the reservations lining her words. "I just don't want you to get swept off your feet by the wrong person. Men with that kind of power can be… persuasive."

"Not Cole," I said firmly. "He's not that guy. I promise, you'd like him if you met him."

"I just don't want you to get hurt." I appreciated my mom's concern, but it was unwarranted and right now, I wanted to focus on relaxing and letting this spa day take the edge off all my stress.

"I'm not going to get hurt, Mom." I sighed and wished I could just hang up.

Another pause, then a resigned sigh. "Alright. I'll trust you. But if he does anything that makes you uncomfortable, you call me right away. Got it?"

"Got it," I promised, smiling. "Love you, Mom."

"Love you too, sweetheart. And enjoy the spa. You deserve it. I'll call you tomorrow to talk about Aunt Sally. Now probably isn't the time."

"Bye, Mom," I said, realizing she probably just wanted to gossip about something her sister had done. I was relieved that I was actually busy and unable to sit here talking the whole time.

I hung up, setting the phone aside as Lena pressed into my shoulders again. The tension was uncoiling, and I put my phone down on the massage table beside me.

I wondered if what they said had any merit. Mom only wanted what was good for me, and she was telling me the same things Alana had, but I still didn't believe her. Was I just blind? Was it that I was being ignorant because I just liked him? Or were they just too closed-minded?

I finished my spa day, choosing to buy a sexy negligee from the boutique in the front of the spa, then I sat in the waiting room, waiting for Cole to pick me up. I might have miffed last night by drinking too much, but tonight he and I were going to have a good time.

17

COLE

I had our cab drop Rose by the spa with a promise to return in three hours on the dot, then I headed out toward the clinic where I'd see the specialist. My hands were shaking, but not because of the tremors. I clenched them into fists and flexed them, trying to shake away some of the nerves. This wasn't a fatal condition —based on my research—but it would be career ending eventually. I just hoped to stave that off for a while.

I sat in the waiting room for about thirty minutes before they took me back. The nurse was kind enough, checking my vitals and asking simple questions. Every answer I gave made me feel more vulnerable and at risk. There was a voice in the back of my head telling me I was weak for feeling this way, but I couldn't help it. A surgeon with unsteady hands was no surgeon at all.

"Well," Doctor Ballard said as he walked in, "what do we have here?" He narrowed his eyes on my chart and his balding head scrunched up. I wrung my nervous hands together in my lap as he focused on the sheet in front of him. I didn't want to interrupt his concentration, but I was anxious to get this over with. "Dr. Hastings, is it?" He looked up at me and pushed his glasses up to his head, exposing his kind eyes.

"Yes, Cole Hastings. I'm a trauma surgeon out in Denver." I swallowed the knot constricting my throat. "I came here for anonymity." My chest felt tighter than a piano string.

"Yes, we get that a lot," he said, looking back at my chart. "So, you've done no testing yet? EEG, MRI? Nothing?" His eyes flicked back up to me. "Essential tremors seems like a diagnosis you've given yourself. Are you a neurological surgeon?" His skepticism was warranted. I hadn't exactly clarified on the intake form I filled out online that I hadn't seen anyone about this previously.

"No, sir, that's why I'm here. For your expertise. My self-diagnosis could definitely be wrong. I just wanted to give you a place to start looking." I'd done a substantial amount of reading so I knew what I was looking into, but the ultimate diagnosis would come from him.

"And you don't want this reported to your insurance? You're all out of pocket?" His skepticism continued, but he had to understand why I was doing it this way. If I could treat it without telling the board, it would be better. There was too much heat on me already.

"Yes, sir. Insurance is required to keep files..." I left the deduction up to his own mind, and he nodded.

"I understand." He eyed me for a moment and said, "You know if we uncover this condition you fear you have and it's progressed, we might not be able to stop or reverse it. And stress will only make it grow exponentially worse. You won't be able to keep this a secret for long."

The pronouncement was something I already knew, but hearing him say it aloud made me feel like punching something. Life got out of control sometimes, but this was something I never expected to happen.

"Of course, I know that. I just want to do what I can now. It will give me time to get a plan together for my future." It didn't mean I wouldn't be able to drive or work, just that I wouldn't be able to operate.

"Well, I'll be happy to treat you once we get some tests. We'll need a serum copper test to rule out Wilson's disease. We need MRI and CT scans to show it's not Parkinson's or MS. We'll do an EMG, DaTscan, thyroid, tox screen, CBC, and a few other physical assessments. If we can induce a tremor and observe it, we'll know better what we're doing. Can you come back next week for the testing?"

I sighed and gripped the edge of the exam table, controlling the anxiety-induced anger I felt. "Uh, no, sir. I have a full schedule. I was hoping we could handle this today. I just need answers." My mind was racing with what-ifs. I needed help immediately, and I couldn't very well prescribe myself the medications needed. Every prescription was tracked.

"Alright, well sit tight. Do you have a few hours? That's what it will take." His eyebrows went up and I nodded. Then he continued as he stood up, "We won't have any conclusive diagnosis today because the results of these tests take time—up to a week. But we can start you on Propranolol to help with tremors, or Gabapentin, though that might make you sleepy."

"Whatever you think will help right away. I have a few important surgeries this week. I don't want to chance a mistake." The truth was every surgery was important, and I didn't want a mistake on any of them, which was why I was here.

"Alright, be patient while I get my staff prepped. It will take the whole team, but we can probably get most of the testing done today for you. At least the important ones." He smiled and shook my hand, which tremored slightly as I reached for him. He watched it and shook it, then nodded. "I'll be right back."

I waited for another thirty minutes while they prepped everything, but miraculously, they got me out of the office in under two and a half hours. The bad part was I'd left Rose waiting for me after her spa treatment for quite some time.

In the cab on the way to pick her up, I apologized profusely by text message, promising her the best dinner ever. And when the cab pulled up outside the spa, she was waiting on me. She climbed into the car and pecked me on the cheek, all smiles.

"How'd it go?" I asked, pushing away my nervousness. She looked beautiful and relaxed. She had a small gift bag in her hand and her nails were freshly manicured.

"Oh, it was so relaxing," she said, leaning into me. I put my arm around her and tried to soak in the positive energy she was exuding. "My God, I never knew how much I needed that massage. It was such a treat. Thank you."

"You're so welcome. I'm really glad you enjoyed it." I smiled and pressed a kiss to her temple, and she put her arms around me and sighed happily.

"What were you up to?" she asked, and I tried not to tense. I hadn't really come up with a good story for what I'd be doing because I was too overwhelmed by the thought that this doctor could give me very bad news. I felt put on the spot, but a quick, deep breath helped me respond without lying too much.

"I just sort of hung out and lost track of time. I'm just glad to be back here with you... Now, what about dinner? Do you think we should go out?" I was already starting to relax a little by putting the day behind me and looking forward to the evening. I hoped Rose was up for some fun so I could really compartmentalize and forget about my stress.

"I was thinking we could eat in. There's something I'm looking forward to." She looked up at me with a cheeky smirk, and I knew what she meant.

I didn't bring her out on this trip on purpose to put the moves on her, but I figured that two adults in a consenting relationship who were sharing a hotel room would inevitably go there. And I especially liked that she was instigating it.

"Oh, you mean like surf the channels in our huge room with the sixty-inch TV?" I winked at her, and she snickered.

"Yes, that's exactly it." The car hit a bump and she jostled against me, and I held her tight.

"Well, I think I should get our food ordered." I reached for my phone, and she suggested a few places she had looked up while waiting for me. We settled on Indian food, and I placed an order for pickup because the retreatant didn't have delivery. She wanted to be left in the room while I got it, so I humored her, though it would have made more sense just to take her along.

When I got the food and returned to the hotel, I found her dressed in a slinky white teddy, draped across the bed seductively. The curve of her hips up to her ribcage caught my eye first, then her perfect tits, mostly exposed. I set the food down by the door and turned the lock and grinned at her lustfully.

"What's this? I thought we were eating..." I dropped my wallet by the food, toed off my shoes, and unbuttoned the cuffs of my shirt.

"You can eat all you want..." Rose propped herself on one elbow, splaying her other palm on the red comforter. She looked so damn sexy I was swelling instantly.

"All I want? Is this a buffet?" I inched closer, devouring her with my eyes. Her skin was flawless, not a single mark on her warm, creamy complexion. The first time we had sex in my car, I saw barely any part of her. In my kitchen, we were so hasty I didn't take time to admire her, nor had I that night when we were in my room with the lights off.

I felt like I was seeing all of her for the first time, and I was drooling. I wasn't the type of man to be turned on by tits, but hers were perfect—soft, fleshy globes in perfect proportion to her body. And the way her shoulders smoothed down into her collarbone was a huge turn on. I wanted to palm a handful of her ass and squeeze it.

"All you can eat," she said, grinning. Then she rose up to all fours and crawled to the edge of the bed and waited as I approached. Her chest pushed out, but it was the curve of her ass with the G-string riding up it that made my dick go full mast.

I couldn't help myself.

I grabbed her by the waist and pulled her toward me, crashing our lips together. Her mouth was warm, wet, inviting. The way she opened up for me, her tongue swirling around mine, made my cock throb with need. My hands moved of their own accord, up her back and around to cup her breasts. They were heavy in my hands, perfect mouthfuls for me to suck on later.

"Condom's in the drawer," I managed to say between kisses as I broke away to nibble on her neck. I loved the way she tasted, like strawberries. It made me wonder if she bought body wax or something. I knew the spa had a gift shop.

"God, I wish we didn't have to. I want you raw," she moaned, but I knew it wasn't a good idea. I pulled back long enough to undo the top two buttons of my shirt and pull it over my head. Her eyes raked over my chest briefly, as if she were drooling over my toned abs.

Then Rose took the opportunity to reach into the nightstand behind her, which left her ass on display for me. The white elastic riding up her ass was hot, separating her cheeks but keeping her holes hidden. I reached out and cupped her left cheek as I unzipped my pants and freed my dick. I stroked myself and admired her curves.

"I know I'll sound like a perv, but you have a damn fine ass."

Rose snickered and wiggled her hips as I shoved my pants down. No foreplay, no runaround—she wanted me so bad, I could see the soggy spot in her panties from here. I stroked myself a little harder until she turned around with the condom.

"Here," she said, her eyes on my dick. She was practically drooling.

"I got it." I took the condom with one hand and guided her backward on the bed. I wanted her on her stomach, ass in the air, so I could admire that view as I took her, but she pulled me down for a kiss. We toppled down, and I braced myself to prevent my full weight from falling on her. This was better than any drug, the feel of her under me, my hands crushing her tits through the lace.

Rose moaned against my lips as I let go of her breast and slid a finger inside her. She was wetter than I expected, and I couldn't wait to feel that wetness on my cock. I worked her pussy, fingering her, enjoying the heat as it surrounded me and she clenched. But the fabric in the way scraped on my skin and annoyed me.

"This has to go now… It's great to look at, but I want to see all of you." I felt the snap in the crotch of her negligee and tugged. It popped open and exposed her pussy, and she grinned against my lips as I kissed her.

"You just like me naked, don't you?" she purred, and I couldn't disagree. She was sexy as hell.

"I like you any way I can have you, but naked is my favorite right now." Kissing her never felt more right. Any thoughts of my stress or my past—the tremors, my grief, the fear of the future—all vanished when I was here like this with her.

I heard a zipper and opened my eyes to see her undoing the side of her teddy. She pushed the fabric aside and exposed her breast, and I rose up so she could slide it the rest of the way off. Breakaway snaps and zippers were now my favorite parts of her clothing because they let me have easy access to what I really wanted—her.

"I want to taste you," I told her as I came down on her breast. I sucked it into my mouth and squeezed it at the same time. Her nipple was soft, but it hardened under my swirling tongue, and she hissed and clawed at my shoulder.

"Fuck, Cole," she grunted and arched into me.

I cupped her ass and squeezed, then moved to her other breast. I traveled down her stomach, leaving a trail of soft kisses in my wake. The scent of her arousal was heavy in the air now, and my cock throbbed with need as I eyed her wet mound.

"I want you so bad, Rose," I said, and she moaned.

"I can tell," she said, and she snickered. Her hair was a mess, face flushed from arousal. She was beautiful.

I rested my hand on her thigh, using one thumb to softly touch her clit. She spread her legs, opening herself to me, and I ran my thumb down her slit, parting her lips.

"May I?" I asked, and my eyes traced up over her sexy body to her face.

Rose nodded, biting a lip, and I lowered my mouth to her sensitive folds.

"Oh, God, Cole," she moaned as I flicked my tongue over her clit. Her taste was intoxicating, and I couldn't get enough. One hand on her thigh, I used the other to slip a finger inside her wetness. She was so warm, so inviting, like she was made for me. I enjoyed the way her wetness coated my finger as I added a second finger and she clenched.

"You're so tight," I said, and she moaned louder. I rubbed her and thrust into her. My wrist bent at an odd angle, but it brought gasps and moans from her lips as they hung agape and her eyes rolled back.

"More," she grunted. "Cole, more."

I obliged her, sliding my tongue across her clit faster, and pushed my fingers deeper. She arched up in response, rocking her pelvis against my movements. I could get used to this—to her.

"Cole," she whimpered, and I knew she was enjoying every second of it. So I kept doing what I was doing and I reached down to stroke myself while I did so.

"Oh, fuck," she moaned, and her walls constricted around my fingers. The muscles in her thighs clenched as she came apart in my mouth. I lapped up every bit of her juices, sucking her clit until she pushed me away. Even then, I was eager to stay there with my face buried between her thighs. She tasted too good, and knowing I was making her feel ecstasy made me want to do it more.

"Oh, God... just come fuck me," she begged, and I chuckled.

Using the back of my hand to wipe across my face, I crawled up over her and positioned my dick at her entrance. "Can I just feel you for a second?" I asked, and she looked into my eyes with such trust and nodded.

Rose drew her knees up and spread them, letting me nestle down into her valley. I slid into her so slowly it made both of us grunt in pleasure. She was hot and wet, gripping me and letting me come home all at the same time.

"Feels so good," she whimpered, and I agreed.

"God, Rose, you're so incredible." I kissed her forehead and glided in and out of her gently, but I knew if I stayed here long, I wouldn't want to stop. My lips covered hers, and I kissed her hard. She clawed at my sides as I pushed into her as deep as I could, but I had to pace myself so I wouldn't blow.

Her nails raked my back as she arched her hips, meeting my every thrust. "Cole..." she moaned into the kiss, and I knew she was close again. My hand found her clit, and I rubbed it in time with our thrusts.

"That's it, baby," I encouraged her. "Come for me."

She let out a high-pitched moan, and her body clenched around me as she came. Her pussy milked my cock, and her juices coated my thighs. She shuddered and jolted, and I loved the way her skin felt slicking against mine. I didn't want anything to do with that damn condom. So when she calmed, I slowed almost to a stop. It was agonizing, but she was giddy.

"Have you ever done anal?" I asked, and her eyes looked up at me lazily. She blinked a few times and shook her head, biting her lip, and I asked, "Can I try?"

Rose swallowed hard, but she nodded and I grinned at her. "Fuck, you're so hot. You really want me to?"

"Does it hurt?" she asked, and I shrugged one shoulder. I knew if not done right it could hurt, but God, I wanted her so badly.

"I can make it feel so good you'll come again." Just her agreeing to it put me on the edge again, and I had to stop and pull out or I'd blow.

"Alright," she said, but she sounded hesitant.

She turned over and got to her knees, and I positioned myself behind her. Rose reached back and spread herself, and I rubbed her juices all over, smearing them on my cock, spreading them to her hole. When I put one finger in, she hissed and moaned. The second one drew a yelp of pain so I eased up, going slower. I didn't even have to worry about keeping myself hard. I was so turned on by her letting me do this, I thought I'd blow without being in her.

When her moisture started to dry up, I spat on her ass and smeared it around, then pressed both of my thumbs into her tight hole and stretched her.

"Oh, fuck," she grunted, and she put her head down. "Oh, shit... oh, God, it's... wow..."

I grinned at the way I was making her feel and slid my dick into her pussy for good measure. I knew doing this dry would hurt, and I wanted her to come so hard it milked me for every drop of cum I had.

"You ready?" I asked, and she panted and clawed at the bed. I knew she wanted to come again.

"Fuck… do it," she hissed.

I slid out of her pussy and lined up with her tight little ass. Slowly, I pressed into her, and she screamed. Her fingernails dug into the mattress, and she clenched around me.

"Cole, fuck…" she cried out, and I knew it hurt, but I kept going. Her body was so tight, so hot, and it squeezed my cock like nothing else ever had.

"Relax, Rose," I said, and she did as best as she could. "Good girl," I praised her as she took more of me inside her ass.

"Oh, fuck," she whimpered again, and I reached around to rub her clit as I continued to penetrate her.

"You feel so good, Rose. So tight." I leaned over and bit her neck, sucking hard enough to leave a mark. Her walls squeezed around me in response, and it finally felt like she was starting to like it.

I picked up speed, and her moans turned from pain to pleasure. I reached around again and found her clit. She was so close again that it only took a few swipes of my finger to send her over the edge. Her walls constricted around me, milking me as she came, and I couldn't help but lose it too.

I growled out my release as I came deep inside her ass, every drop of my seed spilling inside her. My dick pulsed, and her body contracted around me. I stayed there as her hips jerked and her ass twitched, and when I pulled out, she gasped.

The food was cold. The room smelled like sex. I was sweating, but it felt incredible. Rose was the best drug. I hadn't felt so relaxed in weeks. Now if the rest of our trip went as well as this, I'd feel like a brand-new man going home.

18

ROSE

My stomach turned just at the scent of the food as I passed by the cafeteria enroute to the exit door. Cole was supposed to meet me for lunch, but he left me a voicemail telling me he had a meeting. So I ate alone, then I threw up everything I ate. I'd been sick for a few days now, unable to keep anything down, and Pat told me there was a flu bug going around.

I had other fears.

Cole and I had unprotected sex in his car that night, and while there really was every chance my nausea was just the common flu, there was also a very high chance it was something more serious. Something that would end up changing my life forever.

I'd been avoiding taking a test because I just didn't want to ruin this honeymoon phase Cole and I were going through. We'd spent every night together since coming home from Kansas City, and I was supposed to go there again tonight, but his ditching me at lunch upset me. Maybe I shouldn't have been so upset, but I'd been feeling irritable anyway and overly emotional about things—another reason to be worried about an unplanned pregnancy.

I checked my phone but hadn't gotten a text or call from him. I wasn't sure what to do, so I headed out the door through the outdoor break area where a bunch of doctors and nurses were huddled, talking. Cole was there too, seated by himself with a paper cup full of what I assumed was coffee, staring out across the hospital campus. He had a scowl on his face and was brooding over something, so I approached cautiously.

Not only were there people everywhere, but he just looked like he didn't want anyone to talk to him. I wasn't as deterred by his mood as I was by the fact that he stood me up, but I wanted to try to keep an open mind and be patient with him. I knew before our trip that he was dealing with something, but he never did offer an explanation and I never pressed him for answers.

"Hey," I said casually, flicking a gaze at the people surrounding us. It wasn't unheard of for me to speak to him, but no one knew we had an actual relationship. For both of our sakes, we had to keep it that way. We really should have been discussing going to HR to report it and follow proper protocol, but when I even dared to bring it up, Cole was adamant that no one should know yet.

He wasn't ashamed of me. He was worried about something. I could read it in his expression, which was why I never brought it up.

"Hi," he said, and his gravelly voice made me wince.

"Is everything okay?" I asked, trying to read his expression, but people were watching me. I kept my distance and a professional look on my face, and he never looked up at me. "I just noticed you sitting here by yourself looking down." I added that to make it seem like this was nothing more than a coworker reaching out to another coworker. My ruse may have fooled others, but it felt so wrong. I wanted to sit down beside him and put my arms around his shoulders.

"Just have to work late. It'll be a late night," he said, and he avoided eye contact. My chest clenched at his words. I didn't know if he was being serious about that or if he was trying to send a message that I shouldn't come to his house tonight. The shock of hearing it almost brought tears to my eyes, though, especially after having worried about why I'd been so sick all day.

"Yeah, that sucks," I mumbled. "Well, I hope tomorrow is a better day for you." I backed away without a response from him and turned my back. My trip home would be sad because the only things I had to look forward to were more of Alana's lectures now.

My head hung as I walked to my car. My phone buzzed, and I figured it was a text from Cole, but I didn't look at it until I was seated in the car and the engine was running. It was nothing more than the words, *I'm sorry*. He added a sad emoji, but he hadn't explained what was going on.

I sent him a question mark in response and headed out. My heart was heavy with worry. I knew based on the interaction we'd had for days now that if it was something I'd done, he would have told me. This was something to do with work, or maybe a wave of grief over his ex-wife. Whatever it was, he would tell me eventually, and I'd be there for him. It just sucked for me in the meantime because I was really looking forward to being with him.

I sighed and dealt with the rush hour traffic, and when I got stuck downtown halfway home, I spotted a pharmacy and an open parking spot on the street. The longer I sat waiting for traffic to move, the more my anxiety needled at my conscience. I ended up pulling into the spot and going into the pharmacy. I bought two tests for good measure and then headed back out.

At home, I was alone. Alana wasn't home from her shift yet, so I slipped into the bathroom with the need to relieve my bladder anyway. I pulled out the tests and peed on both wands, then cleaned up and sat on the edge of the tub waiting.

My mind mulled over the possibility that I might be pregnant, and while it came with so many negative things that might happen, it also made my heart feel slightly happy and alive. The idea of having Cole's baby made me feel full of joy. But the fear of how he'd take it or what it would do to my career also gnawed at me.

Cole and I were so good together, but we really hadn't discussed anything long-term. We were letting things progress at their own pace, which meant we hadn't had any serious discussion about anything yet, not even parenthood or what would happen if I got pregnant. We'd been using protection, but Cole knew that first time *did* happen. I was drunk and we neither one thought to do the right thing. Surely, he would understand this was a possibility.

When I felt like I'd tortured myself for long enough, I reached for the tests. My hands shook as I picked them up and read them both. Double pink lines on both tests meant only one thing. I was definitely pregnant. It was definitely Cole's baby. And I was about to have to give him the shock of his life, right in the middle of whatever it was he was going through.

Tears welled up in my eyes because I knew what this meant. Inevitably, we would be forced to divulge the relationship to HR, and that meant one of us risked being fired—or both. I couldn't afford to go somewhere else right now, and I didn't even know if he wanted kids. This might be the one thing he never wanted and he'd end up breaking it off with me.

It was that fear swarming my thoughts when the bathroom door burst open and Alana stood there in the doorway gawking at me.

"Oh, sorry, I didn't know you were in... Is that a pregnancy test?" she asked before stalking forward. She snatched one of the tests from my hand and gasped, and I hung my head. "Oh, my God, Rose!" I heard the tone before I saw her face, and I blinked out a few tears. "How could you let this happen? I told you to be careful. Why weren't you safe?"

I knew those questions were because she feared me losing my job, but they were insulting. She had looked for a roommate for a long time before me, and I came in as her savior. I never did any of this to screw with her, but it seemed like she thought that was my intention. I could only hang my head and cry.

I was letting everyone down. When I told my mother, she would freak out. Alana was freaking out. Cole was going through something freaking out, and just for a moment, I wanted someone to notice that I was freaking out too. This wasn't in my plan. I never wanted to have a baby this young, but this was my reality.

Alana stood there breathing heavily and staring at me, but I couldn't make eye contact. All I could do was stare at my feet and cry. When I swiped the tears away, I felt her push some toilet paper into my hand and I finally looked up at her. She closed the lid of the toilet and sat down and sighed, and I saw compassion in her eyes.

"I'm sorry. I'm here." She pulled me into her arms and hugged me, and I just kept crying. I wanted things between Cole and me to be perfect, and as much as I loved the idea of having his baby, it also terrified me. What if this destroyed us instead of bringing us together?

"Hey, shh," she soothed, rubbing my back. "It's going to be okay. We're going to figure it out..."

I didn't know exactly how to take this sudden shift from her, but it was comforting, nonetheless. I let her rock me back and forth, and I took several deep breaths before sitting up straight and blowing my nose.

I had no one to blame but myself, so I had to put on my big girl pants and deal with this. Angry or not, I had to tell Cole the truth, and I had to face my mother's disappointment.

"I'm going to hear it from my mother, Alana. I just need a friend right now, not another authority." I sighed and squeezed her hand, and she nodded.

"Got it... No lectures from me. And I'm sorry for being so hard on you, okay? I'm here." She squeezed my hand back, and I met her gaze.

Right now, a friend was exactly what I needed, and I was thankful for having her beside me. This was going to be a bumpy road.

19

COLE

The room was tense before I even walked in. I knew what was at stake. If Twin Peaks thought for even a second that they would be found guilty in this lawsuit, which was definitely going forward now, they were going to scapegoat me. After one nurse spoke up—probably afraid for her own career—saying I was negligent, I knew where this was headed.

I lowered myself into the seat next to my malpractice insurance mitigator. I had shopped around for a good lawyer, but I still hadn't found one I trusted. The hospital's lawyers were sharks, but they weren't defending me. They were defending the hospital against the bad press and the mark to the hospital's reputation. They were decent guys and probably hated what this would do to my career, but they had one job —protect Twin Peaks.

The eyes of several board members never even turned in my direction once. They all knew what they were doing to me, and they all knew it was morally wrong. This hospital system had billions of dollars to back them, hundreds of thousands of men and women employed for them who depended on the work they did every day to provide for their families. I was just one person with my own life on the line, and instead of standing as a rampart between me and my impending doom, they sloughed it off onto my shoulders.

"Mr. Hastings—"

"That's Dr. Hastings," the mitigator corrected, but he didn't fool me, either. He was the man sent by my insurance company, but even he wasn't here to defend me. He was here to mitigate the loss the insurance company would have in the way of payouts because of me. Then they'd hike up my premiums and I'd be unable to pay them or find work anywhere.

"Dr. Hastings," the lawyer for the client said, "Senator Drumb nearly lost his life because of your negligence."

"Alleged negligence." The mitigator wasn't having any of this. "Innocent until proven guilty." His eyebrows quirked up in the center, and for a moment, he sounded like a lawyer, but while he had the liberty to speak on my behalf, he was only truly making sure the insurance company paid as little as possible.

"May I finish?" the lawyer said, scowling at my mitigator. He eyed both of us for a few seconds, and Victor Ronald—dean of medicine here at Twin Peaks—nodded at him to continue. "The Senator almost died. The hospital has gone through their reports of what happened and found that Dr. Cole Hastings' actions were solely to blame for the incident. We have therefore named Dr. Hastings in our lawsuit. We don't wish to destroy anyone, but the fact of the matter is that blame has been assigned and our client seeks damages."

I knew it was coming, but the shock of the truth being announced like this only makes me feel more hopeless. Until that statement was spoken, I still held out hope that they'd see how naming me personally would affect me. Suing a health system as large as Premier Health meant a huge payout for the patient but only a slap on the wrist for the hospital. Suing a doctor meant the patient got his payout, but I'd never be insured again. It meant the end of my career.

"With all due respect, Mr.—" My mitigator stood, but the lawyer cut him off.

"When you say with all due respect, what you mean is you think I'm a moron. Sit down." The lawyer's eyes were on fire, shooting daggers at the insurance agent. "Dr. Hastings, I strongly recommend you acquire counsel for the next proceedings. We'll have a deposition and we're entering discovery. There will be a lot of things to go over, and you will want to get your affairs in order."

I didn't even know what to say. I wanted to scream out in my own defense, but it was pointless. The second Victor named me as the guilty party, they never looked at the hospital again. I know those records never indicated the patient had allergies to medicine or the preexistent comorbid conditions. If I had known that, I'd never have operated, or I'd have done my due diligence to prevent what happened from occurring.

Victor stood and said a few things, most of them deeply apologetic statements directed at the patient, who wasn't in attendance at today's meeting, and the droning sound of his voice made me zone out.

As hard as I'd fought for the past few months to keep my condition under wraps so I could keep my job, it all felt like it was for naught. The tremors weren't even the thing ending my career anymore. It was something entirely unrelated but just as devastating, and it would suck anyone near me down with it.

When the meeting was done, I rose and walked out, feeling like a zombie. The HR woman who warned me to get a lawyer had been right and I just didn't want to believe her. I thought this wouldn't happen, though I feared it would. And while I knew it was a possibility, I wanted to believe the best about people, about the administration of this hospital, but I was wrong.

"Dr. Hastings, wait up." The mitigator scurried after me, and I glanced over my shoulder with a scowl.

"What do you want?" I grumbled, turning down the hallway toward my office. I hated how he appeared to be on my side while underneath, he just had to make sure he did his own job or risk being fired. I was the one with my life on the line while everyone around me turned a blind eye just to save their own skin. It was despicable.

"Sir, we should talk about your deductible. In a time like this—"

"My God, can you just give me a break?" I knew I was being rude, but I didn't care. I was so upset, and this fool only wanted to talk about his job. I'd had it.

"Dr. Hastings, this can't wait." He stopped walking, and I took a few more steps before I stopped abruptly.

I took in a deep breath to expand my chest and push away some of the tension, then I let it out and turned around, gritting my teeth so I could face him and get this over with. I said nothing, which triggered him to begin talking again.

"Sir, the twenty-five-thousand-dollar deductible is due now, before the suit goes to court. Per the terms of your policy, you have to pay that up front. That's your only cost out of pocket, and we'll make sure you're covered on—"

I scoffed, shaking my head and cutting him off. He stopped talking, and I felt like I'd throw my fist across his face. "My only cost? You mean you'll continue to cover me when this jerk demands five million dollars from you on my behalf? That the hospital won't fire me after this? That I'll be employable somewhere else and not lose my license? What good is insurance, anyway? I may as well just file bankruptcy now."

The weaselly man stared at me, and I saw the defeat in his eyes. It was finally driving home to him how much this was going to affect me.

"Sir, I'm just doing my job."

I blinked a few times and shook my head. "Everyone is just doing their job. I did nothing wrong. How's that for doing your job? Those charts were changed after I looked at them, and I had no way of knowing that what I would go on to do would hurt the senator. Do you think I'm heartless?"

My chest was pounding, and I knew if I didn't get my anger under control I was not only going to make a scene, but I would probably have a heart attack or something.

"The hospital has agreed to pay half of your deductible..." He looked remorseful, but his sympathy meant nothing. And their money meant nothing. I could cover the deductible. It was the loss to follow all of this when it was over that was going to destroy me. The hospital's money was just a pity move, aimed at making sure they came out looking good when this was said and done.

"Go away," I told him, and I turned on my heel and walked toward my office. I was glad when he didn't follow me.

When I finally sat down in my chair and rubbed the frustration off my face, I thought of Rose and how this was all going to play out. I felt really sad that only days ago, I was considering going to the board and declaring our relationship to them to avoid our getting called out or fired. She was really nervous, and I just wanted to do the right thing. Now I knew if we did that, she'd end up having her reputation here damaged too. I hated that for her, and I was ashamed. I didn't want to drag her down with me, and I knew by the time this was over, I really would be bankrupt.

All my hard work and dedication to this job since I was twenty-six years old would be for nothing. I was going to lose everything because Victor Ronald had to "do his job". No one would ever hire me again. I'd be the leper among physicians, and where would that leave Rose? I'd end up having to move away from the city just to find a job, and she didn't want to leave here. She just moved here. Not to mention, how would I ever provide for her? What type of man can't get a job and yet still wants a woman to depend on him?

I had my phone in my hand, ready to call her and break it off just for her protection, when someone knocked on my door. I looked up to see Juan poke his head in and offer a concerned expression.

"Is now a good time?" he asked, and I rubbed my face again and shook my head, but he came in anyway. He walked right over and sat down after closing the door behind himself, and I clenched my hands into fists and pounded them onto my desk.

"This is so infuriating!" I shouted, probably loud enough that people in the hallway could hear me.

"I take it the meeting didn't go so well?" Juan's grimace didn't quite match mine, but I appreciated the show of solidarity.

"They're naming me. They said the hospital found me negligent, which probably means the hospital paid the lawyer off to tell his client to aim it at me. They're protecting themselves, and I'll take the fall." I just still couldn't believe it.

"Maybe you should let the lawyers and the insurance work it out. If they go through the files and see that the charts were changed after you already did your consultation and prep for surgery, they'll find you innocent. There's still a chance..."

While Juan may have been right, I just couldn't believe him. Bad things just seemed to follow me around like a dark cloud. On top of that, I'd gone on the record privately about my tremors. If the lawyers started digging into my life—and I knew they would—they'd see the medical reports and know I was hiding something. I'd be subpoenaed to divulge the medical records I was keeping secret, and that would be the end anyway.

"Yeah, maybe," I grumbled, but I didn't really mean it. I was going to lose everything, and what sort of man would I be then? Would Rose even want me anymore? What would this washed-up surgeon even do? I was too young to retire.

20

ROSE

The apartment was very quiet. Alana went off to work for the day, but I called in sick. I stayed home to sulk, mostly, but I was really nauseous this morning, prompting me to be so emotional, I didn't want to see or talk to anyone.

When Alana first walked in on me in the bathroom with those pregnancy tests, I thought I was in for a huge lecture, but she'd turned out to be very understanding. It turned out she had a pregnancy scare a while back that she hadn't told me about. She lost the baby in a miscarriage, but it had rattled her to her core. She put aside her frustration with my risking my job—and her financial security—to comfort me because she knew how it felt to be shocked by that sort of news.

It worked out well for her, despite the emotional pain of losing a baby. She explained how she wasn't ready to be a mother, how the man she slept with was just a loser and they broke it off as soon as she told him. She told me how relieved she was that he just left her because she really thought he wasn't the type of guy to be a good father, then how devastated she was when the baby was gone.

Then she told me how she moved on and realized it was for the best, that she could never have supported a baby. We discussed my options —abortion, adoption, keeping it. I took my time carefully considering each of them. Even now, I was wrestling.

Abortion was off the table immediately. I fully supported other women who made that choice for their lives, but I could never do that. I just didn't think it was right for me. So I lay in bed for hours last night thinking about adoption and how hard it would be to carry this baby to term, then hand it over to someone else. I might not have been ready to be a mother, but I definitely wouldn't survive that.

So after I slept a few hours and woke up to a bad dream about losing my job because someone caught me kissing Cole, I lay and stared at the ceiling thinking about being a mother. I wanted to do something so much better for my children than my mother had done for me, but I was in no financial position to take care of a baby. I barely made ends meet as it was, and I had a great job.

Sighing, I rolled over and picked up my phone. My heart felt like reaching out for something to find comfort and help. Alana had given me great advice, but I just felt restless. She and I had bonded the minute I moved in here, but after weeks of her nagging me about Cole and my job stability, it just didn't feel the same coming from her. I missed my family, especially my mom, and I wanted to hear her voice.

Still, after she'd been surprised to hear that I was dating an older man, she'd been less than enthusiastic. It did take the wind out of my sails. I knew she would be disappointed in my choices and shocked to hear I was pregnant, and I didn't know if I could stand that. At the very least, she'd be worried about me and my future, which really wouldn't be helpful, but I just needed her the way every woman needs their mother.

I dialed her number and put the phone on speaker mode, laying it on the coffee table in front of me. It rang a few times before she picked up, and I could hear a lot of noise in the background.

"Hey, Mom, is now a good time?" I asked, and it was hard to keep the emotion out of my tone.

"Sure, baby, what's wrong?" Just the sound of her voice put me at ease and allowed the emotions I had shoved down to well back up. Tears sprang up to my eyes and I blinked them back.

"Um, I just need to talk to someone and I miss you." I thought of our last conversation and how I was so happy and full of love. She probably thought I was being dramatic or something, but there was no way I could predict this would happen.

"I'm here, baby. What's wrong?"

I paused for a second to make sure I wouldn't start sobbing while I told her, then I took a deep breath and let it out. "Mom, you remember how I told you I'm seeing Cole?"

"Yes, honey... Oh, don't tell me you broke up." She sounded genuinely disappointed for me, but that was just her mothering heart reaching out to me in compassion. If I told her I broke up with him, she'd lavish me in sympathetic phrases and offers to come comfort me, but deep down, she'd be happy. I knew she didn't like the age difference between us.

"No, Mom. Not yet, anyway." I sighed and pursed my lips, anxious about what she'd say. I had to get this off my chest, though. It was tormenting me.

"Well, what, then? Are you alright?"

"I'm pregnant, Mom..." I swallowed hard and closed my eyes as if by doing so I could block out the emotion I felt and the anxiety rattling me in anticipation of her response.

"I see," she said softly. "And you're sure it's his?"

"Mom!" I hissed, frustrated by that. What sort of woman did she think I was? I wasn't just sleeping with random men just because I moved to the city.

"I'm sorry, dear. That was insensitive..." She sighed. "I'm here to help you, honey. What can I do?"

My heart sank about as low as it had ever been, and I felt like all I wanted to do was sleep. But sleeping wouldn't take away what was happening. The only way out was through. I had to face this head on.

"I'm scared, Mom. I don't know if I can do it." My lip quivered, and I blinked out a few tears.

"Honey, every mom who ever found out they were pregnant thought the same thing. Why don't you come home? Your old room is still available, and I can help you through all of this. You don't have to do this alone. And I won't pressure you to do anything you don't want to do. You need your mother during this time."

As good as that sounded, I knew I couldn't do that, at least not until I spoke with Cole. If he wanted this baby with me, then that was the only thing I wanted. I wanted him and I wanted it to work out. But there was this niggling fear that he would freak out and be upset with me. It wasn't like I planned this, but what if he thought I had? I hadn't exactly stopped him from fucking me with no protection.

"What about Cole?" I sniffled and wiped my eyes. "What if he's angry? What if he doesn't want me anymore?"

Mom hummed in sympathy, and it made me cry harder. "Rose, you haven't been dating that long. It's not like you can even tell if there is a good enough foundation for a relationship to be forever. You are not going to be one of those stupid women who rush off to marry a man just because you get pregnant. You need to be with him for love, not because of this.

"If he's not man enough to understand that you need time to process this, then he's not the man for you. You should talk with him about it, but you shouldn't make a decision on whether to be with him or alone until your emotions are stable."

I listened to what she had to say, and I felt like she was being really honest with me and not trying to sway me one way or the other. It was good advice. I should stop and process my emotions about the relationship with Cole separately from my thoughts about mother-hood and doing this alone. I just didn't want to run home and isolate myself while I did that.

"And if I decide I want to come home six months from now?" I asked hesitantly.

"Your room will be here, and so will I..." Mom was quiet. I felt like I was hurting her.

"And if I decide to stay with him? If he wants me and this baby?" I held my breath as I waited for her to respond. She took a few seconds, and I feared what she'd say because every woman wants her mother's approval.

"Then I'll be here and support you, Rose. No matter what. I know you didn't plan this. I can't imagine how scared you are. If you just want to come home for a few days and rest, or if you don't want to come at all, I want you to know I love you. And I'll be here for you, no matter what." The way she repeated that last line put me at ease.

This wasn't how I saw this conversation going, but it made me feel a bit more secure about things. If my mom was on my side, then it didn't matter in the long run whether Cole wanted or didn't want me. I knew I would get through it. My future was changed forever, anyway. A baby tended to do that. So if I had to pack up and move home, I'd just readjust my expectations and move on, no matter how difficult it would be.

I just wanted it to be easy. Except easy didn't seem to be in my future.

One thing was for sure. I did need to tell Cole. I'd have to make a plan to do that as soon as possible.

21

COLE

The whiskey was room temperature, just the way I liked it. I found that having a drink seemed to stop the worst of the tremors, which seemed to be a little worse lately, though I could've been imagining it. It wouldn't help me during surgery, anyway. No one wants a half-drunk surgeon operating on them.

And the beta blockers Dr. Ballard prescribed weren't helping, either. I'd been on them now for a few weeks, way long enough for them to kick in, but the stress of everything happening with the lawsuit was just counteracting any benefit they had. I knew stress levels were contributing to the tremors, but there was nothing I could do.

Ever since the insurance mitigator got involved and I hired a lawyer, I'd been useless. I'd taken way fewer surgeries and even used a few PTO days just to keep my head clear. I knew I was drinking more and avoiding Rose too, but my mood had gone from optimistic and hopeful to downright angry and depressed. I hated being railroaded like this and there was no easy fix.

I sulked, pouring myself another drink and staring out the back window at the rabbits hopping around the patch of clover under the

SILVER FOX'S TWIN SURPRISE

shade tree. Life had been so simple just a few months ago. It was insane how quickly things changed and grew very dark. It felt like spring, when everything was bright and sunny one minute and two minutes later, the storm of the century could come along and destroy everything. That was what I was going through.

I sank onto a kitchen barstool and stared out the window blankly. Alcohol made my head swirl, and I found it easier to think while I was sitting. Juan had been encouraging me to let the lawyers fight it out, but I'd done my own bit of digging. To someone who had no computer background or ability to dissect files or programs, it appeared the hospital was right—that I had fucked things up badly.

But I knew what I saw. I was dead set that when I looked over those files, they never contained the specific information that would have made me feel cautious about the surgery. I tried to remind myself that the important thing was I knew I wasn't to blame, and the senator was still alive. Those were the top priorities, but they didn't matter if he still blamed me and the hospital wanted to make it my fault. I would still lose everything, even if my conscience was clear

The whiskey called to me, begging me to fill my glass again, but I paced myself. It was only four in the evening. Rose was supposed to come by tonight, but I wasn't in the mood. I knew how grumpy I was and I'd been pushing it away, hiding it from her. I didn't know if I could do that tonight. Wearing a mask when emotions were this heavy was next to impossible, and she didn't deserve my bad attitude.

I pulled my phone out and thought about calling her to cancel, but she told me she had something important to tell me, something she was excited about. I heard the tone of her voice, too—nervous happiness. I didn't know what it was she wanted to tell me, but I knew no matter what her good news was, I wouldn't be able to celebrate with her and I'd feel bad.

But I decided not to cancel anyway. Seeing her might very well be what I needed to get my mind off my own problem and think about someone else. Kate used to say that—that when I was feeling down, helping someone else was the way to get out of it. She was wise like that, and I never did understand that until she died. I was forced to go back to work far too quickly, and thinking of it as helping others was really what helped me move on.

The doorbell rang, and I sighed. I hated that I felt like going on autopilot and forcing my feelings down was an obligation, but I knew it was. I couldn't let Rose see me falling apart like this. I needed to be strong for her and I didn't want her asking questions. If she knew I was the reason the entire hospital was up in arms with a threat of job cuts, she'd never think of me the same way again.

Rose deserved someone to care for her, and I'd never be able to do that without a job. If the lawsuit didn't get me, the tremors would, and I'd be no good to her at all. I refused to be a deadbeat sitting on a couch letting his partner earn the bread for the household. I just had to figure out how to fix this. Fast.

I stalked to the door trying to shove the monster into the closet of my mind, but the alcohol made it harder. When I pulled the door open, Rose looked concerned almost immediately.

"Come on in," I grunted, and my head swirled. I waited for her to walk in, but she paused only a few steps inside the doorway and looked up at me.

"Are you okay, Cole?"

My eyes were a bit blurry, the last glass of whiskey really catching up to me since I got up and moved around. I blinked hard and nodded a few times, and she splayed her hands on my chest, leaning in to kiss me.

"Are you drunk?" she asked, and when she lowered from her tiptoes back to flat feet, I scowled. I never meant to hide the fact that I'd been drinking, but her words sounded more like an accusation than a question and it annoyed me.

"So what if I am?" I hissed, and I pushed the door shut and turned back toward the kitchen. She stood there for a few minutes as if shocked by my words, and with my back to her, I winced at my own stupidity.

I wanted to keep this whole thing away from her to avoid stressing her out, and I was off to a horrible start.

"Sorry, yes. I'm a little stressed, so I'm drinking to help alleviate that. Do you want a glass?" I stopped by the island where my glass remained perched on the bar next to the stool I was just seated on, and I picked it up and turned to her.

She had a worried look on her face and shook her head, so I walked over to the liquor cabinet on the other side of the open-concept space and poured myself another glass. I overdid it. I knew I did, but I was too stressed to care. I just wanted this whiskey to knock me out until the stress of this event was over and I could go back to normal—if there even was a normal to go back to now.

"Cole, are you okay? Is there something wrong?" Rose's soft tone made me feel bad. I was clearly failing at hiding my emotions from her, and I knew she wanted to help. The thing was, she couldn't, not even if I told her everything. She couldn't stop the tremors or clear my name, and my unloading this on her would only push her away from me, make her embarrassed to be seen with me, and drive a wedge between us. She shouldn't have to carry my weight.

"I'm fine," I growled, and I picked up the glass and downed it in one swallow. The minute it was down my throat, I knew it was a bad idea. I was already feeling it and she'd just gotten here. The chances of my passing out were very high, and while that was what I wanted, I really didn't want it in front of her. It made me that much angrier at myself, and I scowled again.

"You don't look fine, babe." Rose walked up to me and pressed her hand on my cheek, and I turned away, clenching my jaw. I didn't want to talk to her. I just wanted her to understand that this was my burden and I wasn't planning to tell her about it.

"I said, I'm fine." I removed her hand from my face and backed away, but I was wise enough even in my drunken state to keep my hand from the whiskey bottle.

"Okay..." she said in a half-hearted tone. "Well, do you want to sit down and talk?" When she asked me that, my gut reaction was to snap. I felt rage well up and make my chest feel like a balloon was expanding inside it. I just told her I was fine, but the whiskey was clouding my judgment.

"No, I don't want to talk about it." I felt bad for biting her head off, but I'd just told her I was fine.

"I meant about my news..." she said, sounding hurt. I watched her lower lip quiver, and she backed away. I felt like a fool, and my heart sank. The last thing I wanted to do was hurt her, and I'd done it anyway because the alcohol made me misunderstand her.

"Rose, I'm—"

"Stop," she said, holding her hand up. Her eyes welled up with tears and she backed away another step. "It's obvious you're going through something and you refuse to talk to me. Where I come from, when you're in a relationship with someone, you don't keep secrets."

"Rose..." I followed as she took off toward my front door, but I swayed as I walked. Not eating lunch and then following that by drinking was a bad choice. I was getting wasted way too early.

"No," she spat, stopping and turning toward me. "I thought we were going somewhere, but I'm not sure what to think about this." Her hand gestured up and down from my head to my feet, and she shook her head. "Call me when you're ready to pull your head out of your ass and have a transparent relationship."

SILVER FOX'S TWIN SURPRISE

She opened the door and walked out and slammed it behind herself, and I stood there watching out the front window as she stormed down the driveway and climbed into her car. The only thing in my life that seemed to be going right was now going horribly wrong, and I wasn't sure how to feel about that.

I stood there feeling hollow for a while before turning back toward the liquor cabinet to get another drink. I hadn't meant to hurt her and I hated myself for that, but maybe this was for the best. I was a sinking ship, and Rose just caught the last lifeboat before I started sinking. I didn't want her going down with me, anyway. I just hoped I hadn't damaged her permanently. She deserved good things, not trauma.

22

ROSE

The pile of tissues next to me was larger than the tissue box from which I pulled them. I'd been crying a lot more than was healthy, but pregnancy emotions just got to me. I wasn't fond of the morning sickness either, though that had been manageable. I ate some dry saltines before I got out of bed like my mom suggested, and it seemed to help.

I curled up into a ball on the couch and looked at the TV screen where the movie Alana and I were watching was paused. She was sort of my stand-in partner for the moment. Rick had said some hurtful things about me, and she asked him to keep his distance from the apartment for a few days while I dealt with my heart being broken. Right now, she was around the corner at the drugstore getting some more tissues and a pint of ice cream for each of us.

I hadn't spoken with Cole in two weeks. At plus or minus eight weeks pregnant, I knew there was only so much longer I could go without telling him—because I felt like I was already starting to get a baby bump—but I didn't know how to bring it up. He hadn't been around when I stopped by his office, and he hadn't responded to my texts asking if he was okay, either.

When I showed up at his apartment thinking we would have a discussion about the baby and I'd get a sense for whether he wanted it or not, he bit my head off. I could see he was battling something every day that week, anyway. He was taking off work, showing up late, and I was shocked to find him drunk when I showed up at his house for dinner expecting to tell him he was going to be a father.

Now I didn't know what to do. Cole was going through something and so was I. The problem was that I was more than ready to be vulnerable and honest with him, but he didn't seem to want the same thing. The words Kiki said came back to haunt me. I wondered if this was what she meant by the fact that he didn't want to open up to anyone. Maybe he would never open up enough to trust another woman with his heart and what he was feeling again, and maybe it was never going to work between us.

That thought made me cry harder, just as Alana walked back into the apartment with our ice cream and my tissues. She was used to seeing me cry now, and she assured me that she understood my plight. Being pregnant was a huge step for any woman. Being pregnant when you were single was massive. But with my getting pregnant, knowing she depended on my income to support her as much as I did, and knowing my mother was hours away, my boyfriend couldn't be what I needed right now, and fear over losing my job?

"Hey," she said, sitting down next to me. She'd stopped by the kitchen to grab two spoons and she handed me one, along with a pint of cookie dough ice cream.

I tore the lid off and plunged my spoon into the ice cream as tears streamed down my face. I had no clue why I got myself into this mess. I should've listened to Alana to begin with. She may have been wrong about Cole pressuring me or manipulating me because he was older and wealthy too, but she hadn't been wrong about protecting myself.

I wasn't stupid. I knew that things could potentially end up not working out. No relationship was one hundred percent guaranteed, even marriages. Everyone had arguments. Every relationship took work and compromise. I just didn't think I'd end up pregnant and regretting my choices so early on. I thought I had time to process things and make good decisions, and getting drunk one night was just a huge mistake.

"Hey, it's gonna be okay, Rose." Alana took a bite of her own ice cream and tried to encourage me, but I knew she was wrong. It wouldn't be okay. I had a doom and gloom stamp on my forehead. I attracted bad Karma wherever I went, probably thanks to my rebellious teenage years. Mom always said they would come back to haunt me, and look at me now.

"How will it be okay?" I asked through a mouthful of ice cream. "I'm going to have to do this on my own, Alana. What will happen when I have to take a few months off when I give birth? What then?"

"You could still do adoption or..." Her sentence faded away before she said it, and I knew what she was thinking.

"Termination isn't an option." I offered a stony expression and she nodded. "And how could I ever carry this baby to term and then give it up? My heart would never be the same." There was a good chance she couldn't even understand me because I had ice cream in my mouth and I was crying, but she offered a soft smile and patted my knee.

"Then I'll help support you."

Her weak attempt at making me feel better was failing. I could see how much she cared and wanted me to feel encouraged, but she couldn't do this on her own. That was the reason she put that ad in the paper for a roommate. How would she do it while I was on leave, and how could I begin to pay the medical bills? Not to mention the fact that she didn't know thing one about raising a baby and Mom wouldn't exactly be comfortable staying here for any amount of time.

"I might have to move home," I said, and the sobs rose up before I could choke them back. I didn't want to move home. I wanted to stay in Denver and work at Twin Peaks. It was something I had strived toward for months before finally getting the interview. It felt like life was falling into place for me, and now it felt like life was falling apart just as quickly.

"Oh..." she said, sighing. "But I feel like we just found each other." Alana touched my leg again and her shoulders drooped. "You know how long I've wanted to have a close friend like you? I don't want you to leave. I'll just get a second job or something to save up for while you're on maternity leave."

The emotion in her voice made me cry harder. I hated this. I wanted my life to be normal without disruptions. I wanted Cole to figure out whatever it was he was going through and help me with this. If he supported me, I wouldn't have to move back home and leave Alana alone. I wouldn't have to feel like I was doing this entirely on my own, either, and I wouldn't be freaking out.

"I don't know, Alana. I need my mom, I think. I've never been pregnant or even thought about it. I don't know what to expect or how to feel. You have to understand... You'd want your mom around too." I frowned as I shoved more ice cream in my mouth and tried not to think about all my hopes and dreams going up in flames.

Alana set her ice cream down and reached for the unopened tissue box and tore the plastic wrap off it and opened it. She handed me a few and kept one for herself. I didn't even realize she was crying until she dabbed her eyes, and I felt horrible. This wasn't just going to affect me. It was already affecting her too. My poor choice one night in the back seat of a car was going to upset everything in my life and the people I cared about.

* * *

The next day, Alana came home from work early. I took the day off and slept in. I made my first sonogram appointment to make sure my little guy was doing okay, but it came with heavy emotions. It shouldn't have been my roommate and practically new best friend driving me to the appointment. Cole should've been here. He should be the one supporting me, but he was too busy with whatever stress it was weighing him down to even have a conversation with me.

"You ready?" Alana asked as we got out of the car and headed into the clinic. She held my hand and squeezed it, and I looked her in the eye nervously. I wasn't ready, but I didn't get a choice. Time marched forward without restraint and I was struggling to keep up.

I nodded, and we walked in. I didn't even have to wait for a few minutes before the nurse called us back. She led us to a small exam room with a single table and a machine with a large computer screen.

"You can set your purse there," she said, gesturing at the counter, "and go ahead and climb up there. You'll want to undo your button on your jeans and pull your shirt up." Her smile was cheery.

I imagined she was probably used to doing this test on mothers who planned their pregnancies and who had their partner with them. I felt sick in the stomach over it, wishing Cole were here, but I just knew if he was too stressed to deal with his own life as it was, he'd never manage this on top of all of that.

I climbed on the exam table and lay down, unbuttoning my pants. Then I pulled my shirt up over my belly, exposing it to the chilled air of the air-conditioned room. Alana stood by me with her hand gripping mine and smiling down at me reassuringly as the nurse approached with gloved hands.

"Are you two ready for baby to come?" she asked happily, and I winced.

"Uh, we're not together," I told her. She was probably used to that too, and that made Alana snicker. "The father isn't in the picture." My eyes threatened to well up as I made that pronouncement. It felt like the deathblow to any hope I had of Cole finally reaching out to me and trying to make things right after he bit my head off.

"Oh, I'm sorry about that. You never know these days," she said, placing the wand on my stomach. The gel she applied to the end of it was cold, making me shiver, and almost instantly, we heard a faint heartbeat. "Well lookie there. This little guy is happy to see you."

The nurse turned the monitor so I could see the distant outline of a baby's head and body. I wasn't great at making out the rest of the image, but I could see the round head and smiled. It wasn't scary at all. It was exactly how I pictured it and it started to warm my heart. I was going to be a mom. It was something I always wanted, just maybe not like this.

Alana squealed quietly and patted my shoulder, and I couldn't help the smile creeping across my face. It was a sweet moment hearing the heartbeat for the first time. I thought I would feel more scared or nervous, but it was beginning to calm me down as I accepted that motherhood was in my future.

"So, can you tell what it is?" Alana asked, and I looked up at the nurse's expression of surprise.

"Uh..." she said, looking down at me with a huge grin.

"So, can you?" I asked too, suddenly curious to know whether I'd have a boy or a girl.

"Well, I can't tell you the sex but I can tell something else." Her grin only got larger as she pointed to the monitor. I was curious, so I watched her fingers. "See this dark spot?"

"Yeah," I told her, squinting. It felt like she'd zoomed out.

"And this one?" she said, moving her finger to another spot on the screen.

I didn't understand what she was saying but suddenly, I didn't feel so good. My eyes focused and unfocused as she finagled the wand and suddenly, I thought the heartbeat was echoing.

"Two?" Alana said softly.

"Yes, two. Ms. Williams, you're having twins." The nurse's statement took my breath and left me heaving. I turned over the side of the bed, and Alana darted out of the way as I threw up.

Twins?

It hit my chest like a ton of bricks and I choked on my own vomit. I couldn't have twins. I could barely wrap my mind around one baby. How would I ever do two at once? This couldn't be happening. I needed Cole—now.

23

COLE

My feet shuffled on the blacktop as I bounced the ball. I felt weak, probably dehydration and fatigue. I'd been drinking more, which made me sleep less and stress more too. I hadn't taken a surgery in a week. Rose hadn't responded to any of my messages in days. I was full of anger and out of whiskey and I knew if I didn't stop, I was going to do permanent damage. I felt worse than I had days after Kate died with no outlet for the stress.

"Ya game's off!" Juan said, swiping the ball from me. He dribbled effortlessly around me and took a shot. The ball soared through the hoop and hit the net with a swoosh, and I scowled again and jogged over to the baseline to pick up the ball.

"Shut up," I growled, sick of his taunting. He'd been picking on me over my lack of coordination today, and I hated it. I wasn't a sore loser at all. I just had too much on my mind and I'd been drowning my emotions in alcohol instead of dealing with them, which only let them bottle up. I couldn't help it that they chose today to start leaking out.

I felt my hand shake a little and tried to ignore it. The tremors had been worse this week than last, though over the weekend they were a little better. But I slept most of the weekend away. After meeting with my lawyer who had zero update on the lawsuit except to say the patient had the right to continue or drop the thing, I just felt angry and out of control. It felt like my life was hanging by a thread on the whim of some man with power and money who could destroy me, and I couldn't even plead my case.

The worst part was the one person in the world who I knew could help me refused to speak with me because I'd hurt her, and Juan had no clue the depth of the anger I felt. He wanted to understand, but unless he walked in my shoes, he'd never know. He had never known loss like me. He didn't know what it felt like to have something you love ripped away from you. I watched Kate slip away and I had no control over it. Now my career was taking the same dive and I was helpless to stop it.

"Yo, you alright?" he asked, and I bounced the ball at him. He caught it and bounced it back, and I caught it, but barely. My hand twitched, and I flexed it and clenched it, then shook it out.

"I'm fine," I spat, and I started dribbling. It felt good. I had my back to Juan, whose chest was pressing against me. His arms were extended to either side, attempting to block me from turning. I pushed backward, keeping the ball going with one hand as I peeked over my shoulder and glanced at the hoop.

"What's wrong, old man? You slowin' down?" This sort of trash talk was what I did to him normally. I was okay with it because it was just part of the game, but I had to bite back my negative responses because I knew anything coming out of my mouth would not be fun, playful things. My tongue was hateful because of my anger.

I gritted my teeth and backed into him harder, and he put a hand on my back, pushing me slightly. I had taken at least twenty shots and missed every single one of them because every time I pushed my hand into the air, it twitched. Most of the shots hit the rim and bounced away, but twice they went far left. This time, I was determined to make it.

I glanced at the basket again and turned quickly, leaping on one foot as I thrust my arms upward with the ball. It soared in the air and slammed into the backboard before bouncing wildly out of control and rolling off the court, and I screamed out a curse word in anger. Juan laughed and shook his head. He jogged over to pick up the ball, and when he came back and bounced it at me, I took it and threw it hard at the fence.

"Damn, man. What's your problem?" Juan scowled at me and took a step forward, and my anger got the better of me.

I took two steps toward him and put both of my hands on his chest and gave him a shove. He stumbled backward and came at me in a huff, thrusting his chest against mine and facing off. His chest heaved and his forehead touched mine as he squared his shoulders and puffed his chest out on mine.

"The fuck?" he asked, and I almost shoved him again, but I clenched my fists and gritted my teeth.

"Just back the fuck off, okay?" We stood there face-to-face in a show of dominance until I broke. I knew if I kept it up, I'd punch him, and he was my friend. I didn't want to destroy another relationship because my stress level made my temper flare.

I backed away and walked over to the bench, parking my angry ass next to my duffel bag. I ran a hand through my sweat-soaked hair, and it dripped to the pavement below me as I leaned forward and rested my elbows on my knees.

Juan went after the ball and then walked over toward me and sat down a few feet away from me. He put the ball on the ground between his feet and matched my pose, except my head was hanging and his hands were folded together.

"I get it, Cole, you're going through shit. So talk to me." The way he reacted to me wasn't what I expected, but I didn't hate it. I just didn't know what to say. Telling him what was going on wasn't going to change anything at all. It just let someone else in on my shame.

"What do I say?" I asked, bobbing a shoulder. I raised my head and stared out over the park. People were running and walking on the trails. The sun beat down on the entire area, baking us with its heat. Children laughed and giggled, and there were even a few dogs running around. Everyone else was enjoying life while I was strug-gling to exist under the weight of everything going on.

"Well, start with whatever is making you a cranky old bastard," he said, and he chuckled.

I didn't know what was bothering me most—the fact that I was being sued for almost killing someone, the tremors that were definitely going to end my career as a surgeon, or the idea that I might have destroyed the one pure thing in my life right now.

"How?" I asked, and I looked at him. He nodded his head. Juan wasn't a stranger to trouble or stress, but he just had no clue.

"It's the lawsuit?" he asked, and this time, I nodded.

"Yeah, well that and some other things. I don't stand a chance, and it feels like I don't even get an opportunity to speak my mind." I sighed hard. "My career will be over. That's twenty-plus years of hard work down the drain because Victor Ronald has to protect a billion-dollar machine that employs him." I shook my head and hung it.

"Yeah, that's shit," he said, and I heard the resignation in his tone. Even he knew that what I was going through was shit. No one should have to suffer this. It was the reason we had assurances like malpractice insurance and contracts. In the grand scheme of things, however, it was every man for himself.

"I take it your lawyer doesn't hold out hope?" Juan's question made me cringe. The lawyer never had hope. He told me we'd just settle and lessen the damage, but I wasn't going to concede. I'd done nothing wrong. I was fighting this.

My hand shook a little, so I clasped it together with my other one and rolled my neck a little as I responded. "I'm fighting it no matter what they say, Juan. I just wish I had someone in my corner..."

My eyes caught on the bench just outside the basketball area where Rose had been seated the day I first approached her seriously about dating. Juan pushed me a little, made fun of me a little, and in the end, she'd agreed to join me for a smoothie. How different my emotions were that day from today, and I wished I could reverse time to that moment when the chemistry between us was so thick and real.

Now I'd kill just to hear her voice. I hadn't realized how much I'd come to depend on a smile from her or bumping into her during work, her laughter at my stupid jokes or the way she always had something encouraging to say. I really screwed up when I snapped at her, and I regretted it the minute I woke up from being passed out that night.

"Well, I'm not gonna lie and say there's anything I can do, but I'm here to talk. It can't be easy what you're going through."

Juan's utter lack of ability to help me only frustrated me. I couldn't blame him, but I didn't want to sit here feeling like he just pitied me. I stood up and grabbed my bag.

"Look, man, I'm not feeling up to this. You'll have to play solo today. I'm gonna go home and shower." I hung my duffel bag on my shoulder, and he stood up and shook my hand. The handshake turned into his pulling me against his chest and slapping my back hard once.

I nodded as I backed away and he said, "Call me if you need to vent. We can go for a drink."

I touched my fingers to my eyebrow in a mock salute, but I knew I wouldn't. I had to quit burying my feelings with alcohol or I'd end up addicted to it. I fought out of that hole once after Kate died, and I wasn't going back. I couldn't.

I went to my car and climbed in, and when I sat down, my phone rang. I dug it out of my bag, hoping it was Rose calling me, but it was just the insurance mitigator. I sent it to voicemail, but the over-whelming urge to hear her voice hit me and I just had to try calling her again. I dialed her number, and it rang through to voicemail and I left another message for her, hoping this one would be the one she'd respond to.

"Rose, it's me... Cole. Please call me. I'm sorry for being a jerk. I miss you, and I was hoping you'd be free to talk for a while. I could use a friend."

That was the most honest I could be with her and still keep my privacy. I didn't think I could really feel good about opening up and telling her yet, but I needed the reassurance that we weren't completely over. I didn't want to lose every good thing in my life all at once. God knows, I'd never survive that.

24

ROSE

I got his messages, all twelve of them. Thirty-two text messages too, but after learning I was pregnant with twins, it was me freaking out now, not him. Cole was ready to discuss whatever it was he was going through, but I was afraid, for my career and for what he'd say. He was clearly stressed about something, and telling him he was going to be a father twice over all at the same time just didn't seem fair.

Not only would he have more weight on his shoulders, but the stress of whatever it was he was dealing with would only make him more on edge. He wouldn't be thinking clearly when I gave him the news, and it would make him react differently than if he were calm.

I just didn't know how much longer I could keep it a secret. I told my mother about the twins and she was thrilled. She wanted to come to Denver immediately and help me prepare, but I told her to wait. Alana and I had several discussions. It was obvious I couldn't raise twins in that little apartment, and she insisted that we could find a bigger place. This entire thing really brought the two of us closer as friends, but I felt like a dead weight. If a normal mom took six weeks off work after birth, what would I do?

I stood in the elevator rising toward the third floor pediatrics and dreading my work shift. I hadn't been as sick lately, and at eleven weeks the doctor told me that was unique, especially with twins. Mom credited her protein smoothie and I credited the depression. I missed Cole. I missed the unique chemistry we had and the connection that seemed so strong, like it'd been established by fate long before we even met.

I missed the smell of his skin and the way he told stupid jokes. I missed his laugh and the way he cradled my cheek when he looked into my eyes. It'd been weeks since we spoke, and even though he was trying to reach out, I just couldn't.

The elevator doors opened and I walked out onto the floor. The nurses were huddled around the nurses' station with giddy expressions. Pam and Ginny were somewhere else now. I'd requested to be on second shift instead of first so I wouldn't run the risk of bumping into Cole at all, and so far, it was working, but it meant getting used to a completely different set of coworkers, though Kiki was here.

I strolled up, ready to get my charts and do my rounds, and Kiki grinned at me and nudged me with her shoulder as I reached for the filing cabinet.

"Did you hear the good news?" she asked, and she waggled her eyebrows at me. The other nurses were so happy right now, but I didn't care. There was something weighing me down that even their good news couldn't change.

"No," I mumbled, trying not to sound like a complete spoil sport. I just wanted to focus on getting my job done and keeping my head down. Then I had to go home and make some tough decisions. I had exactly twenty-one weeks to have a full plan for my future, and the likelihood of my having to move back in with my mom was so high it felt crippling.

"The hospital isn't making cuts. The lawsuit that was pending isn't going through. The patient isn't going to sue Twin Peaks or Premier

Health." She beamed and clapped a few times, but even the elimination of that bit of peripheral anxiety I'd been carrying wasn't enough to lighten my mood. I sighed and nodded.

"What happened?" I asked, but I wasn't actually interested in hearing the answer to the question. I just didn't want her to think I was a complete jerk for not caring. Yes, it was a good thing for all the nurses and I was happy about that. Pam was probably over the moon that she wouldn't have to do my job, but I'd end up giving my job up, anyway. They'd just hire someone else to do it.

"Well, it's bad news for Dr. Silver Fox, that's for sure." One of the other nurses whose name I didn't know spoke up, and at the sound of Cole's nickname, I jerked my head up, suddenly needing to know.

"What's that?" I asked, and I took a step toward her, swallowing the instant knot in my throat. I didn't understand how the lawsuit being dropped had anything to do with Cole or why it was a good thing for us. How could I ever think of benefitting from something that would harm him?

"He's the idiot who almost killed the patient. The hospital board found him negligent and the patient is suing him instead. So we get to keep our jobs." I winced as the nameless nurse insulted the man I loved and shook my head, backing away. My hand went to cover my mouth, and Kiki looked at me with confusion.

"Are you okay?" she asked, and I felt so sick I might throw up even though the last time I'd actually thrown up was days ago.

"Uh, fine," I told her, glancing at the clock. It was only a few minutes after four and if I hurried, I might make it to his office on time. I knew the reasons now that he'd been so overwhelmed and ready to bite my head off. He was getting sued for malpractice and I never put two-and-two together. I felt like a total idiot.

I turned abruptly, ignoring the fact that I had a job to do, and rushed to the elevators. I rode it down to his floor and burst out of the

139

carriage as soon as the doors opened. The messages he left played in my mind on repeat. He'd said he needed a friend, and I ignored them because I was afraid of what my secret might do. Now definitely wasn't the time to tell him about twins, but I felt so bad for leaving him alone while he was suffering like this.

His light was on in his office, and his blinds were closed so I couldn't see in, but I knew he was in there. I didn't even knock. I opened the door and walked right in and saw him collecting his things as if he were ready to leave.

"Rose?" he said, surprised to see me, and I shut the door behind myself and shook my head as I walked up to him.

"I'm so, so sorry, Cole." I touched both of his cheeks and almost felt like crying. "I had no idea." Any thought of my stress or worries was gone, and all I was thinking about was him.

"Sorry?" he asked, and he looked confused.

"I know. The nurses told me. I'm sorry I haven't been here for you." My eyes searched his expression as it softened, and then I pressed a kiss to his lips. "Why didn't you tell me?"

Cole's forehead furrowed and he put his hands on my hips. "I didn't want you to think less of me. I guess I ended up making that happen anyway, huh?" His eyes were stormy, and I smiled at him.

"I don't think any less of you, and I want to hear it all, but right now I need you to know how sorry I am. If I'd have known, I'd have been here." I kissed him again, not even caring whether someone walked in. I knew how precarious our situation was, and even more so now that it was complicated by his lawsuit and my secret, but when someone you love is suffering, you do what you have to do to help them.

"I'm sorry I couldn't tell you," he said softly, and I kissed him again.

His nearness overwhelmed my better senses. I needed him more than he knew, probably as much as he needed me but hadn't been able to tell me. Being so close to him again made me feel weak, like if I didn't get closer to him, feel him against my body, I wouldn't ever feel whole again.

"I miss you so much," I told him as I kissed him again. Each kiss was a plea, a desperation to fix this for him, for us, to undo our arguments and his stress, and my worries, and make it all go back to normal so I could feel whole and we could move on. I kissed him harder, pulling him down against my mouth with such force our teeth clashed.

Cole got greedy too, pulling me against his body and crushing his lips against mine. It was like we forgot where we were or what we were doing. Like our separation had only made our need for each other grow stronger by the day until now, the detonation looming on the horizon would meld our souls together forever.

I couldn't pull away, couldn't catch my breath. I slid my hands down his neck to his shoulders and used the leverage to push him toward his desk. He moved willingly, though he was stronger and could've resisted, and I found myself on the edge of the solid oak, legs spread so he could stand between my knees.

"Here and now?" he asked cautiously, and I nodded before kissing him again.

"I need you. Don't make me wait." My begging fueled the fire, and he didn't disappoint.

His hands found the hem of my scrub top, lifting it up and over my head before discarding it on the floor. His eyes raked over me, and I couldn't help but blush. It had been a while since my body had been appreciated like this.

"You're beautiful," he said quietly, his voice full of amazement as he unhooked my bra and removed that too. My nipples hardened in the cooler air, craving his touch.

Cole lowered his head, kissing down my neck, sending shivers through me. His hand moved between my legs, brushing across my wetness and proving just how much I ached for him. He groaned against my skin as his fingers teased me through the thin fabric of my scrub bottoms and panties.

"I need you, too," he growled, his voice rough with desire.

Cole's words sent a delicious warmth coiling in my belly, and I whimpered in anticipation. He had me on the edge of my seat, literally and figuratively, and I couldn't stand it any longer. I reached for his scrubs, desperate to rid him of them as well. His hands were just as impatient as mine, and together we managed to undress each other in a flurry of fabric and frantic gasps.

Cole picked me up, hands under my thighs, and I wrapped my legs around his waist. He sat me back on the desk, not stopping his kisses as he stepped between my legs. I guided him to where I needed him most, and with one deep, satisfying thrust, he filled me. Any other time, I'd have asked him for a condom, but he was so into it, and I knew the worst had already been done. I was already pregnant with his babies and he didn't even know it. I let him slide into me and just enjoyed the sensation of his skin gliding into mine.

"My God, you have no idea how badly I've needed you. Don't ever do this again. We belong together." His growls against the skin of my neck as he nipped and sucked made me shudder and cling to him. His hands gripped my hips, then one slid up to cup my breast. He kneaded it and tweaked my nipple, and I gasped as I hooked my ankles behind his waist and pulled him in deeper.

"My God, baby, I'm so sorry. I'm so very sorry." All I could do was apologize for not being there for him when he needed me most. I felt like the worst girlfriend in the world. I'd let his bad mood push me away and I never stopped to ask why he was so upset.

"Mmm," he moaned on my shoulder, then he sank his teeth in as he kept thrusting. His dick felt amazing, like I hadn't had sex in years, and I was already on the edge. He'd always known just how to make me come, and apparently, that hadn't changed.

"Cole, I love you so much." It came out as a whimper and a moan as he picked up his pace. His hips slammed into mine with a force I didn't know he was capable of. The action made my coil unravel in delicious waves, and I spasmed and clamped down around him as he thrust his dick into me over and over.

My fingernails dug into his skin. I bit down on his chest to stifle my moans, and his hands pulled me harder onto his dick so it hit my back wall and made me jolt. The orgasm was incredible, and I never wanted it to end.

Cole picked me up and sat down in his chair, not even breaking the kiss between our lips. He continued to thrust as he relaxed backward and arched into me. His dick felt so good inside me, and I knew I'd miss it when he did pull out.

"Cole," I whispered into his ear, and I heard him grunting. His body shuddered, his cock pulsed, and I knew he was coming. He buried his face in my neck and groaned as I felt his warmth fill me up.

When his thrusts slowed, his lips claimed mine again. I was late for my shift, dripping with his cum, and wanting to cling to him. We had a lot to talk about, but something told me we were going to be okay.

"I have to go to work..." I said regretfully.

"Call me. Please..." He sat up, kissing my chest softly, and I breathed in his scent. "I want to see you tonight."

"I will." I reluctantly tore myself away from him and used tissues from his desk to clean myself up. We both dressed and made plans to talk later that evening on my dinner break, and maybe if I wasn't too exhausted, I'd go to his house tonight. And then I slipped out.

What was good news for me was bad news for him. I wasn't sure what to think of that, but I knew we would figure it out together. At least I knew what he was going through now, and it gave me the patience I felt I needed to keep my secret a bit longer. The lawsuit wouldn't last forever, and maybe this was a sign that keeping my secret wasn't a horrible thing. Maybe we'd make it after all.

2 5

COLE

Rose walked out of my office, and I sank behind my desk. The way she swept into my presence and took me by surprise literally changed my entire perspective on things. My hand trembled as I reached for my bottle of soda to have a drink. I had a few more things to finish up here at work before heading home, but reuniting with her had made my day.

We had a short discussion, limited because she was starting her shift, and I felt a lot better about things. She told me she'd heard about the lawsuit and she felt bad for not understanding. It was my fault. I hadn't been open or honest with her, and I never gave her a chance to be understanding or supportive. I had underestimated her ability to see me in a good light. I thought she'd be judgmental, and I realized how judgmental that was of me to think that.

Despite the lawsuit and the tremors, I sat there with a stupid grin on my face. Rose Williams was really the most amazing thing to happen to me in the longest time, and I was an idiot for ever thinking otherwise. Yes, she had seemed guarded, but I knew we were taking a huge risk by even being alone in my office together, let alone having sex at work while we were on the clock. I knew people had been fired for less, so I tried not to read too much into it. If she wasn't going to hold my bad attitude against me, I wasn't going to hold her standoffish behavior against her.

I walked out of my office to finish a few last patient checks with a bounce in my step. She would never be able to understand how much it meant for her to be in my corner. She didn't even know all the facts, but she fully supported me and promised it wasn't something that would separate us. There was still a bit of anxiety rolling around inside my head over the hand tremors and what she'd think, but I tried to push that away. Thinking of that made me worry about my future again, and I wanted to stay in my happy place.

I visited Mrs. Whitaker, a patient who saw a different doctor, but his vacation conflicted with her recovery. I volunteered to check up on her, and she was doing fine. Then I checked on Mr. Fischer who had a hernia surgery done in an emergency situation. I felt a bit useless at times since I was refraining from snagging surgeries, but I knew until my specialist and I got a follow-up, it would be difficult for me to hide the tremors. I made do by helping others, and right now, I was flying under the hospital board's radar.

When the patient visits were up, I checked the time and realized I only had a few minutes left until my checkup. Dr. Ballard and I had scheduled a video conference for this evening, and I was anxious to update him on the status of my tremors. I turned toward my office and made sure to lock the door when I stepped through the door. This appointment was crucial to helping me maintain my confidence.

I logged on to my computer and waited. About three minutes until I was scheduled to join the teleconference, I got an email with the link. I ran a hand through my hair and clicked the link, and my computer joined the session. Dr. Ballard's face appeared on my screen, and I turned the volume down to make sure no one outside my office could hear.

"Dr. Hastings, how are you doing today?" Dr. Ballard smiled at me, but I was too nervous to smile back.

"I, uh... I'm doing alright. You?" My hand shook a little, and I tucked it under the desk and clasped it together with my other hand.

"I'm well, thank you. I have all the results back from your imaging and blood work, and I'm not surprised to have to tell you there isn't anything conclusive here. How have you been feeling?" His words didn't surprise me, either. Despite wishing there would have been some easy diagnosis for this and a quick, easy treatment—no matter how painful—my gut told me this would be the case.

"I'm doing okay. A little stressed at times, and worried, but I'm in good health." That was a total lie, but what was I supposed to say to the man? The words "little" and "stress" didn't belong in the same sentence.

"Good, I'm glad to hear that. What about the tremors? Are the beta blockers working?" He raised his eyebrows expectantly, but I had no good news for him. It was soul crushing to admit it, but the most basic treatments weren't working.

"My tremors haven't gotten any better. I hate to say it, but the stress level is affecting me. I drank for a little while, but I realized that wasn't good and I stopped. The tremors are a little worse now, and I'm not happy about it." Being honest about this was my only option. He couldn't help me if I lived in denial. He was a specialist who saw this all the time and treated it. If anyone could help, it was him.

He frowned at me and nodded as if accepting his own defeat with the initial treatment option. "Well, we can try another beta blocker, but in my experience if one doesn't work, none do." He sighed and looked back down at whatever it was in his hand, then back at me. "We have a few options, but they're not great. They'll take you out of the game for a while."

That was exactly what I didn't want to hear. Between the trip with Rose and the time I'd been off due to freaking out and calling in sick, I had no more paid time off to use up. I had to save a few days for around the holidays and even then, I'd be pushing it. But I wanted to know his options.

"What are they?"

"Well, we can do some deep brain stimulation, but it will take a while to recover from that. Or there is a new treatment with Botox, but it's not promising yet." He rubbed his face and looked thoughtful. "But let's try these new beta blocker and see what they do. I'd like you to try a yoga class or some sort of stress relief. It will definitely help you if you're less stressed."

Hearing him tell me I had to decrease my stress felt like a death sentence to my career. I was living through the most stressful thing of my life. Even losing Kate hadn't felt like this. Sure, some of the pressure was off after learning Rose knew about the lawsuit now, but the lawsuit was still looming. I couldn't just wave my hand and make it go away. Not to mention how stressed I was over these hand tremors to begin with.

"Sure, new beta blockers," I told him, and I knew the other treatment options weren't even options. I couldn't have deep brain stimulation without burning through two more weeks of paid time off, which I didn't have. And Botox was so new, I didn't trust it. I didn't want someone shooting Botox into my brain.

"Alright. I'll call in a scrip to your pharmacy, and you take some time to relax. Let's schedule a follow-up in four weeks, shall we?" He smiled again, and this time, I couldn't even offer a calm expression. I just nodded.

"Yeah, thanks, Doc." I waited for him to disconnect the call, and then I turned off my computer. It wasn't at all the news I wanted to hear, though I wasn't sure that I even expected anything different.

My life really did attract all sorts of negative garbage, and Rose was such a gem for being a part of it. I just hoped the negative things didn't scare her away. I had a feeling I was going to a dark place again, and I knew how it affected her last time.

26

ROSE

I stood over Cole's stove stirring the pot of spaghetti sauce while he stood by the window in his front room staring out at the storm. It was dark, almost like nighttime despite being mid-afternoon, and thunder shook the entire house. I felt like it matched Cole's mood today—like his mood every day for weeks.

We'd made things right weeks ago, but he was still the same grumpy, brooding guy who pushed me away, except now I knew why. I felt sad for him, and more than anything, I wanted to make things right for him, but I couldn't. I knew the lawsuit had to run its course and right now, the lawyers were in discussions on ways to mitigate the damage to Cole's career. I secretly prayed it would go away, but I knew that was a long shot.

"Dinner's almost ready," I called, hoping my cooking would put him in a better mood. We spent a few evenings a week together, but he was always so down, we didn't do much but sit on his couch and watch TV. In fact, I even tried to get him interested in sex those first few days, but he just told me he wasn't in the mood. I'd have thought he was cheating if I didn't know better.

This whole thing sucked. I was okay without having sex, and frankly, now it was a good thing he didn't want to do it. I was starting to show. The twins were making my belly grow at twice the rate of a normal pregnancy, and I already had to wear really baggy shirts to mask the bump I was getting. I noticed the changes to my body, but thankfully, Cole hadn't.

"Alright," he said in a grumble, then he moved away from the window and joined me at the table. I set the pasta sauce next to the bowl of pasta. I set the table earlier and poured myself a glass of juice. Cole had a glass of Scotch. It was his go-to drink now. For a while, he wasn't drinking, but lately, it felt like he always had a drink in his hand when I was over. It was no wonder he didn't notice that I was gaining weight or changing shape. He was always half-tipsy.

"Thank you for letting me cook for you," I told him as I served some spaghetti onto his plate. His eyes traced my movement, and he nodded, giving a curt smile.

"Thank you for taking care of me. I really don't deserve you." He caught my hand and brought it to his lips, and I saw the sadness in his eyes. I changed the subject thinking maybe it was what he needed, for me to distract him.

"So, it's really raining outside tonight." I smiled as a clap of thunder again shook the house, but my topic of choice seemed to be the wrong one. He scowled and plunged his fork into his pasta, twirling a bite on his fork. I winced and looked down at my own empty plate and decided I should eat something too.

I served myself some spaghetti and felt sad. So many times, I wanted to tell Cole about the babies and hope it would cheer him up, but so many times, I stopped myself. If there was even the slightest chance that he would think it was stressful or negative, if he didn't want to be a father or he would be upset with me, I knew I couldn't say it. So I sat paralyzed most of the time, worrying about my own future while he was worrying about his.

"I, uh... I heard from Kiki that the hospital is adding a new cancer research wing..." At this point, I would have talked about Donald Duck just to snap him out of it and help him feel better, but he just grunted and shrugged at everything I had to say.

I took small bites, chewed carefully, and tried not to stress. My blood pressure had already been too high this pregnancy. My doctor was concerned I was stressing too much. I'd done some tests already to determine what was wrong, but nothing was conclusive. The only thing I could tell her was that I was worried about my future. In reality, I was worried about my future, and my job, and my relationship with Cole, and Cole himself.

It felt like everything was out of control and there was no one to reach to for help. I could only imagine how Cole felt about the whole thing. He was tormenting himself with fear of losing this suit and potentially his career too. That in turn trickled over to me in so many ways, but mostly because I was on a timetable. In just a few weeks, my belly would be large enough that I wouldn't be able to hide it from anyone, not even drunken Cole Hastings. Who even knew how long the lawsuit would drag out?

"I'm not feeling so well," I told him after taking a few bites. I really just wanted to go home and rest, but I felt bad leaving him like this. I felt like he was my responsibility and that if he was alone and hurting, it was my fault. I should be here for him. If there was a "him" to be here for.

He looked up at me blankly and nodded, and I saw the glassy-eyed expression he gave me. He was hurting so much, and there was nothing I could do to help him. "You can go home, babe. I'm sorry for being so down."

I felt horrible for wanting to go home, so I sighed and sucked it up. "I don't want to go home, but maybe I could just rest in your bed a while?" I glanced around at the kitchen. It was a disaster when I showed up, so I cleaned it up so I could cook. I knew he wouldn't clean this up either, and it would be waiting on me the next time I forced him to eat a proper meal.

"Yeah, that's okay. I'll finish eating and come check on you." The fake smile on his lips hurt me more than the fact that he had mentally checked out. He wasn't being real with me when he did that, and I didn't even think he realized he was doing it.

I blinked back a few tears and stood up and nodded. I didn't say anything else as I kicked off my shoes and climbed into his bed. I sent Alana a text letting her know I was sleeping over, and she asked how he was doing. I didn't respond. I just curled up in his bed and went to sleep.

Hours later, I was awakened by the bed shaking as Cole climbed in with me. He smelled like booze as he curled around me, and I felt utter defeat wash over me. If something with the lawsuit didn't break quickly, I was going to have to give up. It really wasn't good for me or the babies to keep carrying this much stress. I knew he was going through something, but there wasn't much more I could do, and I needed a break too.

This entire situation sucked. I wanted my mom, and that wasn't a feeling any grown woman ever liked having.

27

COLE

I sat behind my desk with a stupid grin on my face. Either Rose was my good luck charm or life was finally starting to cut me some slack. I set my phone on the desk in front of me, cautious of the time, and breathed a deep sigh of relief. Victor had just called to let me know the coast was clear. The patient who had been hounding me for months with the threat of a career-ending malpractice lawsuit had just dropped the entire suit.

I didn't know what influenced his decision or why he'd decided not to pursue a lawsuit anymore, but it was the best news I'd gotten in weeks. I had to take a moment to breathe it all in and let the feeling soak into every cell of my being. I wasn't going to be sued now, and it was such a weight off my shoulders.

After months of worry and toil, I felt home free, though I did still have to figure out how to handle the tremors I was having in my hands, but that seemed like such a small thing now that the pressure of a lawsuit was off. I wanted to celebrate. I wanted to take the rest of the day off and plan something special for me and Rose to do together that would help me put the last few months' struggle behind me.

I thought for a moment about what might be special. She'd been coming a few times a week to cook for me, but I spent most of my nights feeling worried and stressed out so I hadn't given her the attention she deserved. For a while, she tried to initiate intimacy with me, but I just wasn't in the mind frame to enjoy it. I felt like I'd done her a disservice with the way she was so attentive and caring, and I had just been a lump.

I sent her a message asking her to join me for dinner, and she responded immediately with an affirmative. I told her I had good news, and she said she had something she wanted to tell me too. I wasn't sure what that was about, but I had spent the last few months obsessing about a lawsuit. I wasn't going to spend a single second worrying about what she had to say. Whatever it was, we would work it out and be fine.

Once I knew she was coming, I ordered from a special Italian restaurant and told them to deliver it by five. Then I called and asked my neighbor to use my hide-a-key to come in around a little before four and set up candles and soft music. With everything set up, I sent Rose one more message letting her know if I wasn't there right at five, to let herself in and I'd be there soon. Then I made my way toward the elevators.

Before I even got in the carriage, I was stopped by a phone call. It was my emergency line and the call was from the hospital number, so I couldn't ignore it. I swiped to answer and held the phone to my ear as I pressed the elevator call button.

"Hastings... What is it?" The elevator took a second, and I listened to the nurse as I waited.

"Dr. Hastings, this is Ellen from Emergency. You're the doctor on call this evening. We have a myocardial infarction and we need you in OR One, STAT." As she said the words, my chest tightened and I knew there was no getting out of this. I had passed on so many surgeries, but on my on-call night, there was nothing I could do.

"Yeah, give me vitals..." I stepped onto the elevator the moment the doors opened, and Ellen started rattling off the patient's vitals. It sounded to me like we were dealing with a complete blockage which meant if I didn't do emergency surgery immediately, the patient wouldn't make it.

I took in all the information on my march toward the operating theaters. It meant I definitely wouldn't make it home by five, but if I did well, I could be there by six at the latest. When I approached the scrub room, I shot Rose another text asking her to be patient with me and told her about the surgery, then I ducked into the scrub room and turned my phone off.

The procedure was simple. I'd done angioplasty before, and hopefully, that was it. My scrub nurse helped me get scrubbed in, and I walked into the theater prepped and ready to go. The room was chilled and I wasn't quite prepared for it. Typically, angioplasty didn't require cooling the patient significantly, and I looked up at the monitor to check his vitals. It was only then that I realized I wasn't doing an angioplasty. This patient needed a full bypass.

I knew right then and there that I wouldn't be at the house even by six. It made me frustrated, but I couldn't take time to feel my own feelings. I moved to the side of the table and extended my hand. "Scalpel, please." The nurse passed me the scalpel, and we were in business.

The first part of the procedure went well. I made the initial incision and used the bone saw to cut through his sternum. As I did, another surgeon worked on selecting a vein from the man's leg muscle to use as the bypass. We worked in tandem the way any good team would, and in under three hours we had the bypass in place and I was ready to close the man up. I knew Rose was waiting, but I wasn't trying to rush anything.

As I began suctioning the blood out of the chest cavity, I noticed something horrifying. My hand twitched, and it wasn't the first time during that surgery it had happened. The amount of blood I was suctioning off showed me something had gone wrong and I hadn't even noticed it. No one had noticed it, not even my perioperative nurse.

"Dr. Hastings?" she asked, leaning over the man's open chest cavity. "We have a bleeder..." She turned up the suction slightly and took the hose from me while repositioning the light so I could see more carefully.

I didn't know how this had even happened. I had to have nicked one of the arteries when doing the bypass, and I felt frantic and tense as I packed the chest cavity with gauze and she suctioned off more blood. He wasn't bleeding profusely, but it wasn't something I could leave open. I was so angry with myself.

All the surgeries I had performed like this in emergency situations and never once had I done something so stupid. I silently cursed myself as I located the wound. By the time we found it, one of the other nurses had another needle ready for me. I stitched it shut and breathed a sigh of relief, but the clock read eight p.m. and I knew Rose was probably frustrated with me.

Dr. Grant and I finished the surgery and closed him up, then we waited for another thirty minutes to ensure our patient was stable and ready to be moved to recovery. No one said a thing to me. They probably didn't know what to say. I'd just jumped out of the frying pan, figuratively speaking, and my team knew if what happened got reported to the higher-ups, I'd be right into the fryer. That wasn't something I wanted to even think about happening.

I walked out to the parking garage and got in my car before even turning my phone on. I hadn't gotten any more of a response from Rose via text message, but I missed two calls from her. I knew she was probably upset. I glanced at the clock on my car radio and saw it was after nine. The food was probably long-since cold and Rose might have given up and gone home. I started my car and headed out, setting my phone to use hands-free mode. When I tried calling, she didn't answer. I didn't blame her. I was upset with myself. She had every right to be angry or hurt. I invited her to dinner and then I stood her up.

I drove all the way to my house and parked, and when I didn't see her car, I knew I'd ruined things. I was still relieved the lawsuit had been dropped and I was out of the woods as far as that was concerned, but it did worry me that I hurt Rose and didn't have a way to apologize to her. Leaving a voicemail just wasn't an option. I wanted to speak to her in person.

And the tremor during surgery that led to that artery being nicked had me shaken too. Enough that I knew something had to be done. I couldn't just keep going on like nothing was wrong. If no one reported things this time, I was still running the risk of it happening again, and there was no telling what would happen next time.

I let myself in and walked right to my liquor cabinet, which had been my routine for weeks even after telling myself I had to quit drinking. When I got there, however, I realized how futile that was. Drinking hadn't done anything for me except to help me bury my emotions for a while, and tonight, I didn't want to bury things. I wanted to feel. I wanted to heal my heart and be a better man, a better surgeon.

So I got on my phone and pulled up the website for Dr. Ballard. He had mentioned a few options for treatment that would help me potentially put these tremors behind me for good, and I knew I had to stop pretending I could manage this myself and do the right thing. I was on the right path forward now, and if I ignored this and jeopardized my future, I'd never forgive myself. Rose deserved a man who could take care of her, and that's what I wanted to be.

How could I take care of her if I couldn't do my job? It was time to face the inevitable and get proper treatment.

28

ROSE

The silence in Cole's living room was deafening. I sat on his stupid, perfect couch, the kind that looked like it had never been sat on before, and stared at the clock on the wall. Every tick felt like a slap. He was officially three hours and fifteen minutes late. No call. No text. Nothing. He said he might be as late as six, but I was sitting here past eight p.m. and I'd already eaten alone.

I tried to convince myself that he had a good reason. Maybe his phone died. Maybe he got stuck in traffic. Maybe—oh, who was I kidding? He'd stood me up. For what, I had no idea. But I was done sitting here waiting for him to explain.

The twins shifted inside me, and I felt a sudden, sharp pang of guilt. They didn't ask to be dragged into this mess, into my whirlwind of bad decisions and even worse timing. And I hadn't even thought of how to broach that topic with Cole yet. Not with what he'd been going through. "I know, I know," I whispered, rubbing my belly. "Daddy was supposed to be here by now."

Daddy. The word felt heavy, foreign. And right now, Cole wasn't doing much to earn it. His drinking was out of control. He was always in a mood, and now he was standing me up.

My stomach churned, as if it had decided to team up with the clock in shaming me for sitting here for so long. I needed to rest, but my stubborn streak didn't want to leave before he showed up. Not until I could at least give him a piece of my mind. My body had been through the wringer lately with stress. Taking care of him while growing two babies was taking its toll on me. My blood pressure was too high and I just wasn't sleeping right.

I grabbed my phone again and checked it for what had to be the hundredth time. Still no missed calls, no texts. Just the two voicemails I'd already left him, both unanswered.

"Hey, it's me. Are you on your way?" That one had been hopeful. Naive. He'd never been late, but he never gave me a reason for why he wasn't home. Everyone at Twin Peaks knew he wasn't taking surgeries. I figured it was because of the lawsuit and his stress level. But maybe he just didn't trust himself after drinking so much.

The second one was less friendly. "Cole, where the hell are you? I've been here for over an hour."

I wanted to leave a third just to really drive the point home, but what was the point? He wasn't answering, and I was done feeling like a complete idiot for thinking tonight was going to be special. I planned to tell him. I had a onesie with the word *Daddy* on it to give him, and then another to hand him that said *Mommy*, hoping he'd get the point that there were two of them. Now I didn't even know if I wanted to tell him yet.

"Fine," I muttered, shoving my phone into my bag. My movements were jerky, frustration making my hands clumsy. I stood up, grabbed my coat, and glanced around the room one last time. I left his food in the fridge, my container in the trash to show him I'd eaten. It was kind of him to set up the candles and music, but I shut it off immediately. As I left, I blew each of the candles out and then locked up.

I didn't bother leaving a note. If he couldn't bother to show up, why should I?

I slammed the door behind me and headed out into the night. If Cole wanted to explain himself, he could damn well figure out how to find me.

By the time I got up to the apartment, I was soaked to the bone. It had started raining halfway home, and I'd been too pissed off to grab my umbrella from the trunk. The cold drizzle seemed fitting somehow, like the universe was piling on just for kicks. Like it conspired with Cole to break me further.

The second I opened the door, Alana was there, her face etched with worry. She took one look at me and gasped. "Rose, what the hell happened? You're drenched!" She ushered me in and shut the door behind me, then she grabbed a towel and peeled my sweater off me and wrapped the towel around my shoulders.

I didn't answer. I just kicked off my shoes, dropped my bag by the door, and went straight for the couch. My body felt heavy, like I'd been carrying the weight of my frustration and heartbreak for months instead of hours. The farther along in this pregnancy I got, the more depressing it was. I was supposed to be enjoying these moments, and I just felt guilty for keeping the secret and angry that Cole wasn't what I needed. Which only made me feel guiltier for thinking that while he was struggling.

Alana grabbed another towel from the bathroom and tossed it at me before sitting down next to me. "Did Cole do something?" she asked, her voice gentle but probing. "You were so excited about tonight."

I laughed bitterly, the sound sharp and ugly. "He didn't do anything because he didn't even show up." I dabbed at my pants and peeled my socks off. I couldn't believe how a little sprinkle turned into that downpour, and I managed to step in every puddle in the parking lot.

"What?" Her eyes widened. "He stood you up at his own house? That asshole."

I nodded, rubbing the towel over my head. "I waited for over three hours—almost four. He didn't call, didn't text. Nothing."

Alana reached out and squeezed my hand, her thumb brushing over my knuckles. "I'm so sorry, Rose. That's... awful. He doesn't deserve you." Her sympathetic expression made me sigh hard. He didn't deserve me, but I loved him. And it wasn't that he was being an ass. I was sure of it. I just wished he'd have called me.

"It's not just tonight," I said, my voice breaking. I felt the tears welling up, though that had become pretty normal too. Pregnancy hormones were awful. "It's everything. I can't keep doing this. Between Cole, the twins, my health—it's too much. I've been trying to hold it together, but I can't anymore."

Alana's expression softened, her eyes filling with concern. "What are you saying?" She'd been here supporting me since the moment I took that test and she walked into the bathroom. She knew as well as anyone else how I felt about this pregnancy. She knew I blamed myself for not being careful. And she knew how I'd come to accept it and look forward to motherhood. I just wanted them to have a father.

"I'm saying I'm done," I said, my throat tightening. "I'm quitting my job at Twin Peaks. I can't handle the long shifts, the stress. It's not safe for me or the babies. I'm going back to my mom's house. She can help me, and I'll have time to figure things out." I felt horrible. I knew she relied on my income to pay her bills here, and meeting me was an answer to her prayers. I felt like a bad friend and on top of that, I felt like a failure.

Alana blinked, her lips parting like she wanted to argue, but she stopped herself. Finally, she said, "If that's what you need to do, I get it. I just... I'll miss you so much." Her lip quivered as she spoke, and I knew she was feeling as sad about this as I was, but I didn't have a choice. At twenty weeks pregnant with twins and struggling with health issues on top of that, I needed rest and my mom.

I bit my lip, trying to keep the tears at bay. "I'll miss you too. But I have to put the babies first. I don't have a choice."

She nodded, though her smile was sad. "Rick and I will manage. You just focus on you, okay? And don't forget to call me. A lot." The idea that Rick would move in and help her was comforting, but I got jealous too. I just knew I couldn't do it anymore and I tried not to take offense.

"I won't," I promised, though the words felt hollow. It already felt like goodbye.

After Alana disappeared into her room to call Rick, I sat there alone, staring at the beige carpet like it held all the answers to the mess my life had become. The apartment felt too quiet, the kind of silence that pressed against my chest and made it hard to breathe. The rain outside had slowed, the rhythmic patter against the window the only sound keeping me company.

I attempted to pull my knees up to my chest and rest my chin on them, but my growing belly got in the way. Cole's empty living room flashed in my mind. I'd sat there tonight, ready to tell him about the twins, ready to give him a chance to step up—and instead, I'd gotten nothing. No Cole. No explanation. Just more evidence that I was in this alone.

I pressed my hands against my belly, feeling the faintest of flutters. The thought of raising twins by myself terrified me. Would I be enough? What kind of life could I give them on my own? I was already stretched so thin, my health teetering most days. I couldn't keep working long shifts at Twin Peaks, running myself ragged.

And yet, what else could I do? Cole wasn't reliable. Tonight proved that. If I told him about the twins now, what would happen? Would he suddenly show up with roses and promises? Would he even care? And if he did, would it last? A small, bitter laugh escaped me. I already knew the answer.

I had to protect myself. More importantly, I had to protect the twins. No chasing after Cole, no bending over backward to accommodate him. If he wanted to be part of their lives, fine, but it would be on my terms. And if he didn't? Well, I'd figure it out. Somehow.

I glanced at my phone on the coffee table, hesitating for a moment before picking it up. My hands were shaking as I scrolled through my contacts and found my mom's number. She'd told me I could come back home any time. I'd resisted for weeks, stubbornly clinging to the idea of independence. But I wasn't independent. Not anymore.

The line rang twice before she picked up, her voice warm and familiar. "Rose? Sweetheart, is everything okay?"

I took a deep breath, my throat tightening. "Mom, I... I need to come home."

Her answer was immediate, firm, and exactly what I needed. "Of course, honey. Your room is ready."

29

COLE

The call went straight to voicemail again. For the fifth time today. I clenched my phone so hard I thought it might snap in half. "Rose," I said after the beep, trying to keep my voice steady. "It's me. Please, just... call me back. I need to talk to you. I'm sorry about... everything."

I ended the call and stared at the screen, waiting like an idiot for a text, a missed call notification, anything. Nothing came, just like it hadn't come yesterday or the day before. I tossed the phone onto the couch and rubbed my face with both hands. I needed to shave, but the thought of holding the razor made me wince.

I looked at my hands, holding them out in front of me. They had become my enemies, trembling the same way they did frequently lately. I'd tried the treatments—meds, therapy, even that damn brain stimulation they recommended. Nothing worked. The tremors came and went as they pleased, cruelly reminding me that my body wasn't my own anymore.

The lawsuit had been dropped weeks ago, but I didn't feel free. I didn't feel anything close to normal. Kansas City was supposed to help me reset, give me space to think. Instead, it felt like I'd packed all my problems into a suitcase and brought them with me. I carried it all around on my shoulders again, and it felt as bad as the anxiety over that lawsuit had felt. The one thing I hadn't done was start drinking again.

I shuffled into the kitchen, opening the fridge out of habit more than hope. A few takeout boxes stared back at me, their contents unappetizing and stale. I hadn't cooked in days. Maybe weeks. It was easier to order out, to avoid handling knives or pots that reminded me of what I'd lost.

My stomach growled, but I ignored it, slamming the fridge shut and leaning against the counter. I stared at the cabinets, willing myself to do something, anything productive. But the thought of chopping vegetables or even boiling water felt like scaling a mountain.

Instead, I grabbed my phone again and scrolled through my delivery app. Burgers. Pizza. Tacos. It didn't matter. I picked the first place that looked halfway decent and placed the order. Another thirty bucks wasted, but at least I wouldn't go hungry.

As I waited for the food, I stared at the blank TV screen across the room. It felt like my life—empty, static. Rose had been my anchor in all this, and now she was gone. I didn't blame her. Not really. But if she didn't call me back soon, I wasn't sure how much longer I could keep pretending I was okay.

I stared at my phone again, the delivery timer ticking down in the corner of the screen. Fifteen minutes until the food arrived, but it might as well have been fifteen hours. My gaze kept drifting to the call log—her name sitting there over and over, a painful reminder of every unanswered attempt.

She wasn't just ignoring me. She'd turned her phone off. That hurt more than I wanted to admit. Rose wasn't the type to ghost someone without a reason, and I knew I'd given her plenty. Still, I couldn't stop the gnawing feeling in my chest, the fear that I'd pushed her too far.

What if she didn't want to talk to me? What if she never wanted to talk to me again?

I ran a hand through my hair, the tremors making it hard to focus. She had to call me back eventually... didn't she?

The cab ride to work felt like it took forever, though the driver barely spoke and the streets were clear. I'd debated calling in sick, but what was the point? Sitting at home wasn't going to make me feel any better, and I'd already missed enough time during the lawsuit and my treatments. If I didn't show up, I'd be fired. My hands fidgeted in my lap, trembling slightly. I shoved them into my pockets before the driver noticed.

When we pulled up to the hospital, I hesitated before stepping out. The place felt different, like I was walking into someone else's life. I used to belong here. Now? I wasn't so sure. I'd done everything humanly possible short of having part of my brain cut out, and I'd never perform a surgery again. I couldn't wrap my brain around that. And how would I tell my bosses?

The nurses' station buzzed with activity as I walked in, but it didn't take long for someone to notice me. Kiki gave me a tight smile. "Hey, Dr. Hastings. Good to see you back."

I nodded, not trusting myself to respond. My head felt like it was underwater. My chest felt hollow, and the only reason I showed up today was to see if I could bump into Rose, the way we bumped into each other when we first met.

"It's good to be back." The lie rolled off my tongue easily. "Have you seen Rose Williams?" I hated that I felt so needy that the first question out of my mouth was about her. I was weak.

"Oh, you didn't hear? Of course... You've been out for weeks now. Rose quit. She said she was moving back in with her mom or something. Not sure why." Kiki shrugged one shoulder and sighed. "I have to get back. Good to see you."

She sauntered off as if she hadn't just destroyed my motivation, and I stared at her blankly for a while. Rose left? She just quit and vanished without saying a thing to me?

I walked to my office and sat behind my desk, staring at the paperwork piled in front of me. It wasn't just paperwork, though. It was a mountain of responsibility, every form a reminder of the life I was supposed to be living—the surgeon, the fixer, the guy who had it all together. My hands trembled as I picked up a pen, the slight shake making the simple act of writing my name feel like a chore.

The treatment was supposed to help. That's what they'd told me when I'd agreed to the deep brain stimulation. It wasn't a guarantee, of course—nothing in medicine ever was—but I'd let myself believe it would work, that the tremors would calm, that I'd get my hands back, my life back. But so far? Nothing. In fact, maybe it was worse now. The doctors had warned me it could take months, maybe even a year, to see any real improvement.

And even then, there were no promises.

I should've told Rose. I should've told someone, anyone. But how could I? How could I admit to the people who looked up to me that I couldn't control my own body? That I wasn't sure if I'd ever step into an OR with confidence again? The thought kept me silent, burying the truth under layers of excuses and half-truths. I didn't want her to worry. I didn't want anyone to see how far I'd fallen.

But now, sitting here, the weight of my decisions weighed down on me harder than ever. Rose had quit, and I couldn't help but think it was my fault. If I'd just been honest with her—if I'd told her what I was going through, what I was trying to fix—maybe she wouldn't have felt so alone. Maybe she'd still be here. Instead, I'd pushed her away without even realizing it, too caught up in my own mess to see what was happening.

A knock at the door pulled me out of my thoughts. I looked up to see one of the surgical coordinators standing there, clipboard in hand.

"Dr. Hastings, there's an emergency case. OR Three. They're asking for you."

My stomach sank. My first instinct was to say yes, to stand up and scrub in, to do what I'd spent my whole life training for. But my hands betrayed me, trembling at my sides as if to remind me of why I couldn't. I wanted to. Believe me, it was my deepest heart's desire. But I felt panic as I stood and followed the coordinator into the hallway.

"What's the situation?" I asked, and the coordinator rattled off some stats. "Dr. Hastings, we have a pregnant woman in distress in the ER. Possible placental abruption. They think she'll need an emergency C-section for twins. You're the only surgeon available right now."

My stomach clenched. A C-section. The procedure was straightfor-ward—one I'd done countless times before—but this wasn't a training simulation or a calm, planned operation. This was an emergency. Lives were on the line, and the tremor in my hands hadn't magically disappeared in the last two minutes.

"Can Patel assist?" I asked, grasping at anything to avoid saying no outright. No one knew, but I knew I had to tell them. I knew it was going to cost me my job and I had no backup plan, but I couldn't risk people's lives.

"She's tied up in a liver case," the coordinator replied, her tone edging toward desperation. "There's no one else."

I stared at her, my pulse pounding. If I said no, what would happen to that mother and her babies?

My heart was already pounding, but a call for my name over the PA system made it worse. The possibility of a placental abruption at twenty-four weeks was dire. Every second mattered. I tried to steady my hands by clenching them into fists as I walked, but the faint tremor persisted, a cruel reminder of how little control I had.

When I reached the ER, it was chaos. Nurses buzzed around the trauma bay, equipment beeped, and voices layered over one another in hurried medical jargon. The patient was partially obscured by the flurry of activity, but I caught sight of her dark hair and pale face. My entire body felt the slap of shock.

It was Rose. She was lying in that bed and I wasn't sure what to think.

My legs locked, and for a moment, I couldn't move. My vision tunneled, narrowing on her face, pinched in pain, her hands protectively cradling her belly.

"What—" My voice cracked as I approached. "What's going on? Rose?"

Her eyes snapped to mine, and the look she gave me was nothing short of furious. "Why are you here?" she whined, her voice tight but loud enough for everyone to hear. "Aren't you supposed to be hiding from your problems?" The pain in her tone wasn't just emotional. I could tell she was in distress. I scanned her body quickly and saw no other trauma. My doctor's brain tried to kick in, but I wasn't sure how to push past seeing her belly swollen with pregnancy, a pregnancy she'd hidden from me so well I never even noticed.

The words hit harder than I wanted to admit, too. I ignored the nurses who were suddenly very interested in the monitors and avoided the knowing looks of the surgical coordinator, who hovered nearby. "I'm the only available surgeon," I said stiffly, trying to keep my composure. "What's happening?"

Her lips pressed into a thin line as she winced through a contraction. One of the nurses stepped in to explain, "Suspected placental abruption. Heart tones are borderline. She's only twenty-four weeks, Dr. Hastings. We need a decision."

I looked at Rose, panic blooming in my chest. My hands twitched at my sides, the tremor suddenly impossible to hide. I saw her eyes flicker down to them, her jaw tightening.

"You can't," she said flatly, her voice cutting through the noise. "You can't operate like this. Look at you."

My face flushed. "Rose, this isn't about me—"

"You're damn right it isn't!" she shouted, her voice rising over the hum of the machines. "This is about these babies. Our babies. And me, Cole. Me! Stop thinking about yourself for once and start being the man you should be." She started sobbing just as a woman who looked just like her but older walked into the room with a bottle of water. She tiptoed around me and offered Rose the water.

The room went silent. Every head turned, every set of eyes on me as the words hung in the air. My chest tightened, shame and anger warring for control. She was right, but hearing it, hearing her say that in front of everyone, hurt.

"I can't do this right now," I muttered, stepping back, my voice thick with emotion.

Her face twisted, part pain, part disbelief. "Of course you can't. You never can."

That was the final blow. I turned on my heel and stormed out, leaving the chaos behind me, but the weight of her words followed me, cutting deeper with every step. The coordinator tried to stop me, but I knew between the emotion and the tremors, there was no way I could do the surgery safely.

"Call Patel. Tell her it's an emergency," I growled, and I stormed out. The risk of her having to wait a bit longer was nothing compared to the risk of my causing harm by operating in my condition. I needed a breath of air to think.

ROSE

My back hurt and I was so sick to my stomach and weak, but more than that, I was scared. When I started peeing dark brown, I knew it was bad and Mom drove me in. I lay on the emergency room bed crying, feeling bad about snapping at Cole, but it was the fear talking. Not only was I terrified about what was happening to my body, but now he knew my secret—the one I should've told him about months ago when I first found out.

"Hey, shh," Mom said, her hand smoothing up and down my arm. I was inconsolable over what happened with Cole anyway, but this just took the cake. I never imagined that they'd want to rush me in for an emergency C-section, and I hadn't stopped to think that if they did, it might be Cole whom they'd call.

"He hates me," I mumbled, and I used the back of my hand to wipe my eyes. I'd seen the pain in his expression when he took one look at me and saw me hooked up to all these baby monitors and wires.

Three weeks ago, the last time I saw him, I was barely able to conceal my pregnancy. At twenty-four weeks now, there was just no way. Had I been pregnant with one baby, it would've been challenging but maybe possible. But these twins had my stomach ballooning out now. Even if I wanted to try to hide it, there was no point.

"He doesn't hate you, Rose. He got a shock." I looked up and saw Kiki standing over me. She smiled and rested her hand on Mom's shoulder. Mom sat on the edge of my bed trying to comfort me, but she leaned back as Kiki stood next to me. "I saw him. He just went out for air. I think a few of us suspected you were pregnant, but—"

"My God, does everyone know now?" I was mortified. For so long, Cole and I had fought to keep our relationship a secret, and this wasn't at all the way I thought things would be revealed. Though, I never planned on a pregnancy at all. I pressed my hand to my belly and felt the twins move. They were most active nowadays, especially in the evenings.

"Shh, don't stress yourself out," Mom said, but it was too late. Tears welled up in my eyes again and I sniffed. "There's nothing you can do about that now, Rose. We'll deal with it later."

Kiki squeezed my hand. "Mom's right. Focus on you and the babies, okay?"

"I should've told him, Mom," I said, my voice breaking. "Why didn't I just tell him?" I swiped at my eyes again and shook my head.

"Look, Rose, not everybody knows." Kiki lowered her voice. It was impossible to make sure no one heard us with just curtains to separate exam stations, but I appreciated that she was being more discreet. "The ER staff doesn't know you used to work here." Her voice was almost a whisper. "And I'm the only one who saw that interaction. I think you're fine. I think you should focus on the babies."

"But," I mumbled and turned away from both of them, "he looked at me like he didn't even know me anymore."

Mom rubbed my arm. "He's in shock too, Rose. Give him time to process it." Her touch was comforting, but I was still upset. The good thing was that I hadn't ruined his career by showing up here and then blurting out how upset I was with him. Maybe I'd let that fester a bit too long and I should've definitely reached out to have that conversation, but hindsight was always twenty-twenty.

"Ms. Williams?" I heard, and I looked up to see a doctor walk in. I didn't recognize her at all, but she had a kind smile and was dressed in blues with a stethoscope around her neck. "I'm Dr. Adams, but you can call me Elise. I'm one of the OB/GYNs on call tonight." She looked at the monitor and then at me, and her eyes softened. "I came to discuss what's going on. We've done some tests, and I'm happy to let you know you're not having a placental abruption like we feared."

Mom sighed in relief, but I just blinked at her. "But... the bleeding?" I croaked out. Dr. Adams took a seat on the stool next to my bed and placed a reassuring hand on my leg. Kiki wiggled her fingers at me and backed out, and I took Mom's hand and squeezed it for reassurance.

"It's called bloody show. It can happen in late pregnancy, especially with multiples," she explained, a gentle smile on her face. "It's not as much blood as it seems, but it can be scary. Your cervix is just starting to efface and dilate early, which isn't uncommon either." She patted my leg. "I know this is scary, but your babies are doing fine. Your contractions have slowed, which is good."

The news was both a relief and terrifying at the same time, but it didn't explain what was going on when I peed. I bit my lip as she continued. "Now, the good news is, there's no indication of infection, and your vitals are all stable. You're also slightly anemic, but that's to be expected with twins." She smiled, and I let out a shaky breath. "However, what's going on with your kidneys is concerning. At twenty-four weeks, we shouldn't be seeing preeclampsia, and we're worried about renal failure."

My stomach plummeted. "What does that mean for my babies?" I asked, panic lacing my voice. Mom squeezed my hand again, and I looked at her, desperately seeking reassurance, but her face had gone pale.

Dr. Adams squeezed my leg through the bedsheet. "We have to look at a cesarean, Rose. Your kidneys are struggling to keep up, and your blood pressure is way too high."

"But they're too early," I croaked.

"I know you don't want to hear this, but it's for your health and theirs. If we don't, the risk of complications increases for all of you." Dr. Adams frowned at me, and more tears sprang from my eyes.

"But, I—" I glanced at Mom and saw the fear in her eyes. I squeezed my eyes shut and took a deep breath. This was happening, wasn't it? They weren't going to magically reverse their decision.

"I know this is a lot to process, but we need to move quickly," she said gently. "We're prepping the OR now. Is there anyone else you'd like us to call? Your partner?" she asked, glancing at my left hand, but there wasn't a ring.

I shook my head and my voice cracked. "Just... just my mom. She's here."

Dr. Adams nodded and patted my leg again before leaving us alone. As soon as she left, Mom hugged me tightly. I sobbed into her shoulder, clinging to her.

"Shh, it's going to be fine. We're going to get through this together, okay?" she said, her voice shaking. But I couldn't find the words to respond.

All I could think about were my babies and how close I'd come to losing them. As soon as the door clicked shut behind Dr. Adams, everything hit me all at once. The fear, the heartbreak, the guilt—it all surged up, overwhelming me. My body felt like it couldn't hold it anymore, and I broke. The sobs started deep and wracked through me as I buried my face in Mom's shoulder.

"I can't do this," I choked out, the words muffled and raw. "I can't be a mom... not like this."

Mom held me tighter, her hands stroking my back like she was trying to soothe me the way she had when I was a little girl. "Rose, listen to me," she said, her voice low but firm. "You can do this. You are doing this. Every moment, every choice—you've been fighting for those babies since the beginning. And they're going to know how much you love them because of that."

"But Cole..." My voice cracked, and I shook my head against her shoulder. "He hates me now. I saw it in his face."

Mom eased back just enough to look at me, her hands still framing my face. "Cole doesn't hate you, sweetheart. He's in shock. He just needs time. And as for everyone else?" She glanced toward the curtain that shielded our small corner of the ER. "Let them talk. None of it matters right now. The only things that matter are you and those babies."

I wanted to believe her, but the image of Cole's face—stunned, hurt, confused—was burned into my mind. "I should've told him," I whispered. "I should've told him months ago."

"You can't change that now," Mom said gently. "What you can do is focus on yourself and these babies. That's all that matters."

Before I could say more, the curtain shifted, and Kiki stepped back inside. Her face was calm, but I saw the worry in her eyes as she approached. "Hey," she said softly. She crouched down so we were eye to eye. "You okay? Well, I mean, as okay as you can be?"

I sniffled and swiped at my tear-streaked face. "Not really."

Kiki nodded like she'd expected that. "I get it. But listen, you're stronger than you think, Rose. You've got this." She paused, her gaze flickering to Mom. "I checked in with the nurse. They're moving fast to get the OR prepped, but they'll come grab you soon. I figured you'd want to know."

I swallowed hard, the reality of it settling heavier on my chest. "I'm scared," I admitted.

"I know you are," Kiki said, her voice steady and calm. "But you're not alone, okay? Your mom's here, and I'm here. We're not going anywhere."

The lump in my throat grew, and I pressed my hand to my belly, feeling the subtle shift of the twins moving. For a brief second, everything went still. I felt the tiny lives inside me, so fragile but so real, and I knew I'd do whatever it took to keep them safe.

"I just... I want them to be okay," I whispered, my voice breaking again.

"They will be," Kiki said firmly. "And so will you."

The curtain swayed open again, and a nurse peeked in, clipboard in hand. "We're ready for you, Ms. Williams," she said gently. "We'll take good care of you."

My heart clenched, and my grip on Mom's hand tightened. She squeezed back, her face calm but her eyes glassy with unshed tears.

"You're going to be okay, sweetheart," Mom said. "You're stronger than you know."

I nodded, even though my legs felt like they were made of lead. When they started wheeling me toward the OR, I glanced back at Mom and Kiki, their reassuring faces the last thing I saw before the curtain closed behind me. My fear hadn't vanished, but Mom's love steadied me, and I clung to that as I was rolled into the sterile, bright light of the operating room.

31

COLE

I went straight to the family waiting area just outside the emergency department and locked myself in and paced. I'd been reactionary with Rose when I should've taken a moment to recognize that she was under duress. Several deep breaths helped me start to calm down, but nothing had prepared me for seeing her there struggling.

Twenty-four weeks pregnant? That meant she had been carrying her secret for more than half her pregnancy all alone while I acted like a fool. I was so stuck in my own world, wrapped up in drama and frustration, half-drunk all the time, and ignorant of anything and anyone else around me. I noticed she'd gained a little weight, but I thought it was because of stress too. I never even stopped to really notice her.

And we hadn't had sex in at least seven weeks. When we did, I thought I noticed changes to her body, but she said nothing, and I just wanted to forget everything to be with her. Now all those clues were falling into place. She was more tired. She'd been sick off and on. She refused drinks with me, which at the time I thought was just her wanting to maintain composure to care for me, but even that was me being self-ish. I never stopped to ask her.

And twins? Holy shit.

I ran a hand through my hair and shook my head. Then I walked to the wall and pressed my forehead to it, splaying my arms on either side of me parallel to my body. My hands were fists, my shoulders tense.

Rose carried this secret on her own for at least four months, all because I was being a total jerk. I should have been there for her and taken care of her, and the entire time, she was cooking and cleaning for me and probably struggling emotionally to cope with things. I was so angry with myself.

Her words rang out in my memory. "Be the man you should be." It was exactly what I should be doing. I'd spent the past six months being haunted by things that in the grand scheme meant nothing. A job was just a job, and losing it—while it would hurt—meant nothing if the people around me whom I cared about were hurting. I was an idiot for placing more importance on whether I could perform surgery again than Rose. She deserved better.

She deserved the man she desired. A man who would go to bat for her, care for her, listen to her, and make sure she was safe and healthy. I had neglected it all thinking she was there for me, and in doing so, I was using her, taking her for granted.

Well, not anymore.

A moment of clarity hit me, and it wasn't because the lawsuit had been dropped or because I knew the treatments were never going to work. Rose wasn't a last resort for me. She should always have been my first priority, right from the start. The moment I realized I loved her should have been the moment nothing else was more important, and I had failed her. But I wasn't going to fail her now.

I unlocked the door and went straight to the elevators. I knew what I had to do, though I knew how difficult it would be. Since the moment I found out that it was likely that I'd be sued, Juan had tried to help me prioritize and stay calm. All of his advice seemed foolish for so long because I felt like he didn't understand what was really important. But he'd known all along. He knew a truth I was too blind to see.

Life was more than your job or how people saw you. I should've learned that when Kate died, but I used my job to catapult me back into my real life without her. Then I taught myself that the job would be here even when everyone else left. Now I was left with a broken paradigm that put everyone around me at arm's length just so I could maintain emotional control, and when the job was shaken, it was the people around me whom I needed. Not the work.

The elevator doors slid open when I pressed the button, and I stepped in. They closed around me in silence and carried me to the top floor of the hospital where the board and hospital administration offices were. It was almost lunch time now. It was possible they'd all be out, but I had to do this while I had the nerve or I'd never do it.

I marched right into Victor Ronald's office, and his eyes popped up from the desk behind which he sat. He smoothed his tie and scowled in annoyance at the interruption, but I walked in anyway.

"What is it, Dr. Hastings?" he asked, and I sucked in a breath to bolster my confidence.

"Sir, I have a few things to tell you, and then I have to tend to an emergency downstairs." I hoped to God Rose would still let me come see her. I knew I had screwed up, but nothing was more important to me than this.

"Well, what is it? I'm in the middle of things." His lips pursed, and I swallowed the knot constricting my throat.

"Sir, I want you to know that none of what I'm about to tell you has affected my work in any way, but I know hospital policy and I have to do this." I felt a little nauseous as I said, "I have had a few hand tremors going on lately. Nothing that would put my patients at risk in the past, but the treatments I've sought aren't helping. I can therefore no longer accept surgeries. I know what this means for my job here, but I felt you needed to know."

He looked surprised and even a bit disappointed, but I continued before he could say anything.

"And sir, I've been seeing a nurse who practiced here at Twin Peaks as well." I pressed my lips into a nervous line as a shadow washed over his face but I continued undeterred. "We've been on and off for a few months, and she quit, but I just wanted to set the record straight. I just didn't want to jeopardize my career by confessing this during the lawsuit. Now, I have to go to emergency. The woman I love is going in for an emergency C-section, and I need to be there for her."

Victor was shocked. He sat there in a stupor as I turned on my heel and marched out. I never gave him a chance to respond because as far as I knew, it meant I'd be terminated, though I was sure they'd find a way to make it look Kosher so I couldn't sue. The tremors were enough to end my position as surgeon, and Victor would have no choice. I couldn't do surgery, so I couldn't be a surgeon.

"We'll need to talk about this!" he shouted after me, but I was already at the door, closing it.

My mind was on Rose. She wanted me to take responsibility and be the sort of man she needed, and that was what I was doing. What I should've done months ago.

By the time I got back down to the ER, she was gone. I walked into the exam room where she was and found Kiki standing with whom I could only assume was Rose's mother. Rose looked just like her, only younger, and she was crying softly.

"Oh, Doc... Uh, they took Rose up for a C-section. I was just going to show Mrs. Williams to the family waiting area." Kiki smiled at me politely. I'd seen her and Rose speaking on a number of occasions and thought how nice it was that Rose had finally decided to open up and become friends with one of her coworkers.

"Thank you, Kiki. I can handle this." I nodded at her as she offered a sympathetic look at Mrs. Williams and walked out.

"They said her kidneys are failing..." Rose's mom whimpered and sniffled. "If they don't do surgery, she'll go into renal failure."

I nodded knowingly, but my knowledge of how this worked didn't calm me at all. Losing Rose now after everything else would kill me. "She'll be alright," I said, taking her hand. "We have excellent doctors here."

My words were meant to encourage her, and all I felt was a knife in the chest. I couldn't lose Rose. Not now. *Dear God, make sure she lives.*

32

ROSE

I stirred awake mid-morning. My belly hurt so badly, I was whining and holding it, and Mom was there in an instant, asking the nurse for medication. She offered me water and pushed the hair out of my face. I probably looked disgusting, but moms don't care about that sort of thing.

"Hello, sweetheart," she said with a smile when I finally blinked all the way awake. Whatever the nurse put in my IV helped almost instantly, and the pain diminished rapidly.

"Uh..." I yawned and nodded. "Hi... where are the babies?" My mind immediately went to my newborns. With the obvious bulge of my belly gone, I knew the C-section was over, but a quick scan of my room revealed no bassinets or babies.

"They're in the neonatal intensive care unit." Mom sighed and patted my hand. "We can go see them. They've been there since the surgery." Her concerned expression made me worry a little. I tried sitting up on my own, but my stomach hurt so much.

"Are they okay?" I winced but managed to push myself upright.

"They're okay, Rose. They're just very small and weak. They'll have to be in the hospital for a few weeks. You've been out for two days while your body recovered." Mom hovered by my side and doted on me, and I almost cried. Two days I'd been out? It felt like I just went to sleep.

I glanced around the room and saw a few empty coffee cups, revealing Mom had been here waiting with me. Her purse and jacket were on the fold-out bed, though it was currently in its couch form. And she had a bag of clothing on the floor near the tray table. It was so sweet of her to stay here.

"Your friend Alana stopped by too. She'll come back when you're feeling better." Mom looked around. "Let me get the nurse. We'll see if we can get you a wheelchair to go down to the NICU and see the babies." Mom patted my hand, and I reached for the glass of water next to me on the tray table.

My whole body felt like it had been put through a tumble dry setting in a dryer. I ached and hurt everywhere, but mostly my heart. Seeing that expression on Cole's face destroyed me. I knew it was my fault, too. My reception to his presence while I was struggling hadn't been the best, but I'd made it worse by having kept this secret to begin with. I knew I should've told him. I just thought I was helping and protecting him. Clearly, I was wrong.

Mom came back with a nurse who had a wheelchair, and they got me—very painfully—situated in it. I expected to see my tiny babies in incubators and hooked up to lots of wires and tubes. What I didn't expect was to have them wheel me into the NICU to see Cole.

He was hunched over an incubator with his hand in the side. His eyes were wide with love and affection and he didn't even notice when we entered. A few other nurses gave me wide-eyed expressions and scurried away to give us privacy, and Mom cleared her throat. She didn't act surprised to see him, though, so I wondered what had transpired while I was out.

"I'll leave you two alone," the nurse said, and Mom patted my shoulder.

"Me too, Rose. I'll come back in a few minutes. You two should talk."

Cole pulled his hand out of the incubator and turned to face me. He had an expression of remorse and guilt. He stood there clasping his hands in front of himself and seeming tense, and a thousand emotions washed over me in a spit second.

"Hi," he muttered, but it was weak. He acted like he didn't know how to behave around me, and that was fair. I'd bitten his head off last time we spoke.

"Hey..." I said, turning my eyes toward the incubator. I strained to see inside, but I was too far away.

Cole walked over to me and pushed the wheelchair closer, and I felt gratitude swell in my chest as my tiny babies came into view. Their little bodies were in the same incubator, snuggled together. They had on the tiniest diapers I'd ever seen, and wires really were connected to them at every spot imaginable. I never worked in a neonatal unit before, but it felt heartbreaking. I wondered how nurses did this every day.

"They're so perfect, Rose," Cole said, and I heard the emotion in his voice. He pulled a rocking chair up and sat next to me, and I reached into the incubator and through the gloved hole. I couldn't touch their skin, but it was probably to keep germs out. They were only twenty-four weeks now.

"Oh, my God," I whimpered, and my eyes welled up with tears. They were so small they could fit in the palm of Cole's hand if he picked them up.

"Rose, I'm so sorry," he said, but he didn't look at me. He kept looking at the babies. "I've been so selfish and self-absorbed..." His head hung. "I kept things from you, and you deserved better. I should have been there for you."

My shoulders tensed, and I looked away from the babies to take him in. "Kept things?" I asked, but the shame on his face made me feel so bad for him too. I was the one who had kept things from him. I knew he was wrestling, and I just wanted to protect him.

Cole wrung his hands together and then lifted one up and held it out between us as he raised his eyes to meet mine. I noticed the tremor making his hand shake and shook my head.

"Essential tremors..." he said. "I've been having them for months. They're incurable. I'm going to lose my ability to do surgery, and probably my job. With the lawsuit and all of this tormenting me, I just got so carried away in my own problems that I never stopped to notice you." He reached up and cupped my cheek. "Can you ever forgive me?"

"Forgive you?" I said, feeling incredulous. "I think you need to forgive me. I was pregnant and I just never told you. You deserved to know." I blinked, and tears leaked out of my eyes onto my cheeks. I swiped them away quickly, but he shook his head.

"You deserved a safe place to confess this, and I didn't provide that for you, and I'm sorry." His hand caressed my cheek and he said, "I need you to forgive me because if we're going to move past this and have a future, I need to know that we can work through things."

I didn't know what to say. I felt overwhelmed and too emotional. Some of that was probably my hormones shifting wildly, but part of it was that I felt like I was the one who needed his forgiveness.

"I wanted to tell you so many times, but I watched how much you were suffering. I felt like you'd be more stressed about things. I didn't want to burden you more. I had no idea you were struggling like that." I thought about all the times I'd wanted to tell him, but looking back, I'd still have done the same thing. I cared about him, and adding more weight to his shoulders never felt like the right decision.

"It's okay. I'm here now. You're safe. They're safe, and we can try again." Cole's thumb traced over my cheekbone as he whispered, "I love you, Rose, and I want a life with you. Nothing is more important to me."

I nodded and leaned forward until my forehead pressed against his. After months of uncertainty and fear, I felt like things might actually be resolving. That we might actually have a shot at this. Fears still swirled around my mind like what if he really did lose his job? Where would he work? And who would provide for us if he had no job? But I knew we were both strong and determined people. We'd find a way.

Love always finds a way.

33

COLE

I walked as slowly as Rose needed me to as we moved toward the conference room on the sixth floor. Rose had been released from the hospital yesterday to recover, but the twins were still here, admitted in the neonatal unit. I wished she'd have stayed with me, but she chose to bunk with Alana, her former roommate, and her mother was holed up in a hotel for the time being. They wanted to refuse my help, but I gave the hotel my credit card and ordered that they charge everything to me for Rose's mother.

Today, I was on my way to hear my judgment. After confessing to everything that had been going on, I was nervous that today's pronouncement would be a disaster. I assumed they would terminate me or I'd be relegated to education, or something worse. I did have an offer from the University of Colorado's medical department to act as a professor of anatomy, which didn't disinterest me, but the pay was less than half of what I made now.

Rose had been supportive from the instant we reunited. Her reassurance and affection were exactly what I needed to keep my spirits high over the past week while Victor and the board decided my fate. Today was when I'd learn what they had decided.

"You're scared?" she asked, and as macho and strong as I wanted to be, I couldn't. Any man who faced this uncertainty with a family to care for—children who depended on him—would feel the same.

"Nervous," I told her, but terror was a better word. There was no greater fear I had in life than the ones I loved suffering or my losing them. My future was uncertain, and that fear of the unknown threatened to cripple me.

"It's going to be okay no matter what they say." She patted my arm, but I should have been the one cheering for her. She'd just gone through a major surgery eight days ago and our children were so weak right now. She had so much courage and strength, it amazed me.

I sucked in a breath and breathed out a sigh, trying to get the tension in my shoulders to abate, but I was just too nervous.

The week had been the longest of my life. Every passing day felt like another turn of the screw, tightening the knot of uncertainty in my chest. Rose had been my rock, her quiet strength keeping me grounded even when my own nerves threatened to unravel me. Now, as I stood outside the boardroom, my stomach churned with a mix of dread and cautious hope.

Rose sat nearby, her hands folded in her lap, looking as calm as ever. But I knew her well enough to recognize the slight tension in her jaw, the faint tremble in her fingers. She was nervous too, though she'd never let it show. She gave me a small smile, the kind that always seemed to steady me when nothing else could.

"You've got this," she said softly.

I nodded, even though I didn't believe it. My palms were damp, and my heart was hammering against my ribs. "I hope you're right."

Before I could second-guess myself, the door opened and Victor Ronald stepped out. The dean of medicine had always been an imposing figure, but today, his expression was unreadable. "Cole," he said, gesturing me in.

I glanced back at Rose, who mouthed, *It's going to be okay*. Taking a deep breath, I squared my shoulders and followed Victor inside.

The boardroom was cold, both in temperature and atmosphere. Around the table sat members of the board, ethics committee representatives, and Victor himself. Their faces were serious, their postures stiff. A thick file sat in front of the chairman, its weight a physical manifestation of my mistakes.

"Dr. Hastings," the chairman began, his voice grave. "Thank you for joining us."

"Thank you for seeing me," I replied, my voice steadier than I felt.

Victor spoke next, his tone measured but not unkind. "We've reviewed your case thoroughly, Dr. Hastings. Your actions—both the concealment of your illness and your personal relationship—were serious breaches of protocol. These actions have repercussions not just for you, but for the integrity of the institution."

I nodded, swallowing hard. "I understand."

The chairman leaned forward, his gaze intense. "You took a significant risk by hiding your condition, Dr. Hastings. A surgeon operating under those circumstances is a liability—not just to themselves but to their patients, their colleagues, and the hospital's reputation. And your decision to keep your relationship with Ms. Williams hidden only compounded the problem. Transparency is not optional in a field like ours."

"I understand," I repeated, my voice quieter. "And I deeply regret those choices. I was wrong."

Victor's expression softened slightly. "It takes courage to admit that, Cole. And your willingness to come forward, to confess and cooperate fully during this process, speaks volumes. It shows integrity, even in the face of your mistakes."

A beat of silence passed, the tension thick enough to cut. My heart raced as I braced for the worst.

The chairman exchanged a glance with Victor before continuing. "The board has decided that we do not want to lose you, Dr. Hastings. Your skill, dedication, and contributions to this hospital are undeniable. However, we cannot allow you to continue as a practicing surgeon under these circumstances."

My stomach dropped. "I—" I started, but the chairman held up a hand.

"Let me finish," he said firmly. "We are offering you the position of surgical chair. This role will involve overseeing operations, consulting on difficult cases, and teaching residents and junior surgeons. You will no longer perform surgeries, but your expertise will guide those who do."

The words took a moment to sink in. Surgical chair. Not termination. Not relegation to education without purpose. It was a promotion—a chance to lead, to teach, to shape the next generation of surgeons. I hadn't even dared to dream of something like this.

Victor's voice broke through my stunned silence. "We believe in you, Dr. Hastings. This position reflects not just your skill but our confidence in your ability to move forward from this and continue to contribute meaningfully to the hospital."

My throat tightened as a wave of relief and gratitude washed over me. "Thank you," I said, my voice rough. "I... I don't know what to say."

The chairman leaned back, his expression still serious. "Say you'll learn from this, Dr. Hastings. Say you'll never put yourself or this institution in this position again."

"I promise," I said quickly, meaning every word. "I'll do everything in my power to earn this trust."

Victor nodded, a faint smile tugging at the corners of his mouth. "Good. We're counting on you."

The chairman continued, outlining my new responsibilities as surgical chair—oversight of the department, pay that matched the gravity of the role, and a clear expectation to uphold the highest ethical standards. The words swirled around me, but my mind was already racing ahead. Relief blossomed into quiet joy as I thought of what this meant for my newborn twins—stability, security, a father who hadn't lost everything. And for Rose, this was a chance to rebuild trust, to prove to her that I could rise above my mistakes and be the partner she deserved. For the first time in weeks, hope felt real.

As I stepped out of the boardroom, the weight I'd been carrying for weeks lifted. The hallway seemed brighter, the air lighter, every step feeling like a new beginning. Rose stood up from the bench where she'd been waiting, her eyes scanning my face for the answer she so clearly hoped for.

"They're keeping me," I said, the words escaping on a shaky breath. "They've made me surgical chair."

For a moment, her face was unreadable, then it broke into the most beautiful smile. "Cole, that's amazing!" she said, her voice trembling with emotion. "I'm so proud of you."

"I didn't see it coming," I admitted, running a hand through my hair. "They believe in me, Rose. After everything… they still believe in me."

Her hand hovered near mine before she pulled back, a flicker of restraint reminding us where we were. But the love in her eyes was unmistakable. "Because you deserve it. You've worked for this, Cole, and no one can take that from you."

I couldn't contain my overwhelming feelings of relief and gratitude any longer. "Rose," I said in a hushed tone, "I can't bear to be away from you any longer. Let's move in together, with the twins. Let's truly be a family."

She took a sharp breath, but her radiant smile stayed firmly in place. "Yes," she replied simply. "I would love that."

The past was finally behind us and our future together was brighter than ever. I couldn't help but feel like the world had finally righted itself. And as we left the hospital together, hand in hand, it felt like we were walking into a new chapter of our lives.

34

EPILOGUE: ROSE

The sound of the twins' soft breathing filled the nursery, their tiny chests rising and falling in perfect rhythm. I lingered a moment longer, watching them sleep, before quietly closing the door and heading downstairs.

Cole's house—our house now—still felt unfamiliar in some ways. The furniture was sleek, modern, and meticulously chosen, evidence of his careful attention to detail. But there were already signs of change. A burp cloth draped over the arm of the couch, a bottle drying on the counter, and my laptop perched on the kitchen table amid stacks of paperwork.

I settled in at the table, pulling up the job search site I'd bookmarked. The thought of going back to work filled me with mixed emotions. On one hand, I wanted to contribute, to find my own way forward. On the other, the idea of leaving the twins so soon tugged at me in ways I wasn't ready to examine too closely.

I was scrolling through listings when I heard the front door open. Heavy footsteps followed, and a moment later, Cole appeared in the doorway. His tie was loosened, his sleeves rolled up, and his expression softened the moment he saw me.

"Hey," he said, dropping his bag by the door and leaning against the frame. "How were the twins today?"

"Perfect," I said, smiling. "They napped longer this afternoon, so they should sleep better tonight."

He grinned, running a hand through his hair. "That's good news. And you? What have you been up to?"

I gestured to the screen in front of me. "Just looking at some job openings. Trying to see what's out there."

His brow furrowed slightly as he came closer, pulling out a chair and sitting across from me. "Rose, you don't have to rush into anything. It's only been six months. You've got enough on your plate with the twins and with everything we've been through."

"I know," I said, meeting his gaze. "But I need to feel... I don't know, useful. Like I'm contributing."

"You're already contributing," he said firmly. "This house feels alive because of you. And the babies? They're thriving because of you."

His words made my heart twist in that familiar, warm way only he could manage. I turned to face him and let his hand cup my cheek. He sat down and pulled a chair up closer. Our knees brushed, and he leaned in to kiss me. His lips were soft and I smiled against them.

When I deepened the kiss, his hand pulled me closer. I loved that he wanted to take care of me, but I was determined to do my part. I wanted to find something I could do for a few hours a day until the twins were more active and needed me around more. Then when they went off to school, I'd return to nursing full time.

"Mmm," I moaned, pulling back with a grin. "Is there more of that for tonight?" I asked playfully, and he smirked at me.

"Why wait for tonight?" he said, winking.

My body started to stir, my pulse quickening as Cole leaned in, his lips brushing just shy of mine. But before we could even kiss again, a familiar sound broke the moment—Ember's tiny wail, quickly followed by Astrid's soft cry.

"Duty calls," I said, sighing as I stood up, though I couldn't help the smile tugging at my lips.

Cole chuckled, his hand grazing my lower back as I passed. "They've got impeccable timing, don't they?"

"They're yours, aren't they?" I teased over my shoulder, heading toward the nursery.

The cries grew louder as I opened the door, and my heart softened at the sight of our daughters. Ember's tiny fists flailed in the air, while Astrid had managed to wriggle half out of her swaddle. Their faces were scrunched in tandem, their cries a symphony of newborn need.

I scooped up Ember first, cradling her against my chest as her wails softened into hiccups. "Shh, it's okay, little one. Mommy's here."

Cole appeared behind me, already reaching for Astrid. He held her with practiced ease, swaying gently as her cries quieted almost instantly. "There we go," he murmured, his deep voice soothing. "You've got to stop making me look bad, Astrid, always calming down so fast."

I laughed softly, adjusting Ember in my arms as I moved to the rocking chair. The routine was second nature now—feedings, burping, soothing. Even in the haze of exhaustion, it was a rhythm I loved, a tangible reminder that our little family was thriving.

Cole sat on the ottoman in front of me, holding Astrid close as he watched me nurse Ember. The way he looked at me, with so much quiet admiration, made my chest ache in the best way.

"You're incredible, you know that?" he said softly.

SILVER FOX'S TWIN SURPRISE

I raised an eyebrow, a teasing smile on my lips. "For feeding our baby? I think the bar's a little low, Dr. Hastings."

He shook his head, his smile never fading. "Not just for this. For everything. For being the glue holding us all together. For believing in me when I didn't deserve it. For saying yes."

My throat tightened, but I managed to keep my voice steady. "You're pretty incredible yourself, you know. For stepping up, for loving us the way you do. For letting me take over your pristine house with baby chaos."

He grinned, glancing around the nursery. "It's not chaos. It's life. And it's ours."

I leaned my head back, letting the weight of his words settle over me. There was a time, not so long ago, when I wasn't sure I'd ever feel this —this sense of belonging, of purpose, of hope. Yet here I was, surrounded by love in its purest, simplest form.

Once the girls were fed and burped, we laid them back down in their cribs, their tiny bodies curling into peaceful sleep. Cole draped an arm around my shoulders as we stood there watching them, his thumb brushing gentle circles against my arm.

"They're perfect," he whispered, his voice full of awe.

"They are," I agreed, my voice barely above a breath. "And so are you."

He turned to me, his eyes searching mine. "You know, I wasn't sure I could do this, be a father. But you... you make me want to be better every day."

My heart swelled, the vulnerability in his voice breaking down the last of my walls. "You're already the best, Cole. For them, for me. For us."

He pulled me close, pressing a kiss to my forehead. "I love you, Rose. I don't say it enough, but I do. With everything I have."

Tears pricked my eyes, but they were happy ones. "I love you too. And I always will."

We stood there a moment longer, the soft sounds of the twins' breathing filling the room, a quiet reminder of how far we'd come. The road hadn't been easy, and there would undoubtedly be challenges ahead. But for the first time in a long time, the future felt bright.

Together, we could handle anything. Together, we were home.